Things *Liars* Fake

Nerdy is new sexy.

Sney

sara ney

This is a work of fiction. Names, characters, places, brands, media, and incidents are either the product of the author's imagination or are used fictitiously. The author acknowledges the trademarked status and trademark owners of various products referenced in this work of fiction, which have been used without permission. The publication/use of these trademarks is not authorized, associated with, or sponsored by the trademark owners.

Copyright © 2016 by Sara Ney

All rights reserved. Without limiting the rights under copyright reserved above, no part of this publication may be reproduced, stored in or introduced into a retrieval system, or transmitted, in any form, or by any means (electronic, mechanical, photocopying, recording, or otherwise) without the prior written permission of the above copyright owner of this book.

First Edition: February 2016
Library of Congress Cataloging-in-Publication Data
Things Liars Fake (a #ThreeLittleLies novella) – 1st ed
ISBN-13: 978-1523739530 | ISBN-10: 1523739533

For more information about Sara Ney and her books, visit:
https://www.facebook.com/saraneyauthor/

Prologue

Daphne

"Everyone raise your glasses in a toast," I announce around the high-top bar table, hoisting my wine glass in the air and encouraging the friends we have gathered to do the same. Clearing my throat, I begin. "To Tabitha: the author friend we're here to celebrate! She worked her ass off for many years to get to this point. She took a risk and left her job to write full-time and is proudly publishing her *second—yes second!* romance novel." I put a hand next to my mouth and address our small group in a hushed tone as if I'm telling them a naughty bit of gossip. "And even though she kept it a secret from us at the beginning, we're all so proud of her."

Beside me, Tabitha groans loudly among the laughter. I continue. "Her first book has been in the top 100 for nine weeks and we expect the second to do just as well because my best friend is a wordsmithing genius."

"We are so proud of you!" our friend Samantha shouts.

"So proud!" Greyson—who is dating Tabitha's brother—echoes, raising her glass higher. "Seriously Tab, we're so excited for you... even though you used my *brother* as a muse for your second novel, which I cannot get past." Grey gives a shudder. "Especially where the characters finally do the deed. Did it have to be so descriptive? All I could do was picture my brother and you—horrifying. I will never be able to un-read that scene, and for that I will forever be ungrateful."

My best friend Tabitha, laughs, her blue eyes sparkling with mischief. "Yeah, but we all know the best ideas imitate real life."

I roll my eyes and lower my glass. "But do we have to *know* about it? Honestly. The visuals we could have lived without." Even though her boyfriend Collin is a complete hottie with a hot bod and killer smile whom none of us, if forced, would mind picturing naked in the sack. But of course, I can't say that shit out loud.

That would be tacky.

Tabitha has the decency to blush. Her hands go up in defeat. "I swear I only used Collin to form the male character! I didn't use our *relationship* to plot the book!"

She can't even look us in the eye when she says it, the liar.

We all stare and Samantha's expression clearly asks *'who are you trying to kid right now?'* "You expect people to believe that? The entire second book is about two people who meet at a store; that's you. Then they bump into each other at a party. You. Then he finds out her secret. Also you. You, you, and you. *Your* story. Just admit it so we can finish toasting your success."

A dreamy smile crosses Tabitha's face. "Fine. I admit it. I was falling in love with him, so yes—I might not have done it on *purpose*, but it *is* our story."

"*Finally*. Now, as we were saying: here's to Tabitha, who we all knew would do something spectacular. Thank you for proving us right. We love you and are so proud. Cheers!"

"Cheers to Tabby!"

"Hey," Bridget—an old college roommate in town for the weekend—cuts in. "When do we get to *see* this famous love letter we keep hearing about?"

She's referring to the love letter that my best friend's boyfriend wrote her during a rough patch while they were dating. Tabitha has never shown it to anyone, but did reference it in her new book.

Which, of course, made us all curious.

Tabitha throws her head back, and face palms herself. "Oh crap. I forgot I put that in my book." She laughs the kind of laugh that makes a guy like Collin fall in love with you and write you love letters. Light and airy and full of humor. "Sorry, ladies. The contents of said letter are private."

"Is it dirty?" Greyson wrinkles her nose. "Please say no."

"No! It's sweet. Ugh, just the sweetest. Maybe someday I'll let you read it, but for now I'm keeping it to myself."

"Damn you and your secrets!" I complain. "I showed you the poem Kyle Hammond wrote me last year."

Half the table groans out loud, and Bridget smirks. "Are you *kidding* me right now? First of all, Kyle Hammond is a stalker that works in your office. Secondly, he plagiarized that poem off the internet. Third, it wasn't a love poem; it was a poem about a man's love affair with a married woman."

I scoff indignantly. "It's the thought that counts."

"He's just so adorable I can hardly stand it," Tabitha sighs into her wine glass.

"Who, Kyle?"

"Collin," my best friend sighs again in a daydream, resting her elbows on the bar table.

"Collin? Adorable?" Greyson laughs. "Okay, yeah—my brother is somewhat good looking. But I also remember he and his friends back in high school doing some pretty stupid crap, like toilet papering their friend's houses and leaving dead animals on the front porch that they found on the side of the road. Gross."

"What!" Samantha sputters, pausing with a wine glass halfway to her lips. "Wait. *What*?"

Greyson nods with authority. "Yup, Road Kill Cafe. He and his hockey buddies would use it as their calling card when they'd go TP someone's house. Anything they found on the side of the road, they'd take and put on someone's porch."

"That's so totally disgusting I need to chug this," Bridget adds, lifting her wine glass and pointing it in Tabitha's direction. "You kiss that mouth."

Greyson continues. "Skunks, opossums, squirrels; basically anything dead on the side of the road. Like, who *does* that?"

"I don't even know if I can drink any more of this,"

Bridget wrinkles her nose and stares down into her wine glass. "I think I just lost my appetite."

"Don't say you've lost your appetite, because I'm starving." Tabitha successfully changes the subject, head swiveling around in search of a menu. "I think this place serves food. We should order something."

My stomach and I grumble at the same time. "It probably only serves bird food to go with this wine. Like cheese and dry fruit and crap."

"Whatever it is, we'll just order double."

Not seeing a menu, I hop down off my stool and dash to the bar to fetch one, returning with a few and setting them in the middle of the table. "Have at it ladies."

I crack one open. "Okay, this looks good: brie wedge and warm raspberry compote."

"Let's also do the artichoke dip, and the bruschetta."

Bridget rubs her hands together gleefully. "Yes and yes. And look, they have crab cakes, but you only get three, so we'll have to order two."

"We're going to look like slobs," I say, closing the menu and signaling the bartender with the flick of a wrist in the air, eying our round table dubiously. "Is this table big enough for all this food?"

"Do you care?"

I shrug, the pretty lavender scoop neck sweater I'm wearing falling down off my shoulder. "Well, *no*…"

Samantha pokes me with the corner of a menu. "Because I don't see any guys here about to sweep you off your single feet. We're free to do as we please. This is girl's night."

Disgruntled, I wrinkle my nose. "You're all either engaged or in serious relationships. Being single sucks. Must you point out my deficiencies?"

"I'm sorry, that wasn't my point! I'm just saying..."

Bridget throws her hands up to stop our banter. "Hold that thought. Rewind! A group of guys just entered the building, three o'clock." We all crane our necks to get a good look, Bridget—the only one of us who's engaged—straining the hardest to catch a peek. "One of them is pretty hot."

"Um... what are you doing?" Greyson asks, shaking her pretty blonde head with a grin on her face.

Bridget winks and tosses her long, brown hair with a flip. "I'm scoping them out, of course. For *Daphne*."

The bartender walks over with her stylus poised above her tablet to take our order and Greyson rattles off our selections, adding two more appetizers, along with another round of drinks.

"That should hold us over for a little bit," she says, handing back the menus. "Thanks." The bartender taps away on her tablet before nodding and walking off.

Bridget's eyes are glued across the room, her wineglass poised at her cherry red lips. "What do you think those guys would say if they saw a shit ton of food show up at this tiny table?"

"What guys? Those guys?" Greyson's hazel eyes widen with surprise, and she cranes her head to look around the dimly lit club. "Why are you staring over there so hard? You're engaged."

If anyone should be ogling that hard, it should be *me*.

"Jeez, don't everyone look!" Samantha demands. "Yes, the guys who walked in before. They're at the bar now and totally checking us out."

Surreptitiously, we covertly sneak glances towards

the front of the wine bar. Sure enough, on the far side of the room, seated along the rails, a small group of guys is in fact checking us out, doing nothing to conceal their interest.

One of them even points.

I do a quick count of the math: four of them. Five of us. Unfortunately for them, I'm the only single one in this group. Well, I suppose we could technically count Samantha as single because she broke up with her boyfriend just days ago; her status might be single, but emotionally she's in no place to be picking up guys at a bar, sophisticated clientele or not.

We figured dragging her out tonight and plying her with alcohol would take her mind off Ben & Jerry.

"Crap, they look like they're going to come over." Greyson groans miserably; if there's one thing I've learned about Grey, it's that she might be outgoing and friendly, but despite her stunning beauty, she's modest, private—and hates getting hit on.

I however, do not. And apparently neither does—

"Samantha keeps staring!" Bridget accuses with a scowl. "You're going to give them false hope if you don't knock it off."

"I wasn't staring!" She huffs. "Alright, so what if I was? There's no harm in window shopping."

While they argue back-and-forth, not gonna lie; my ardent green eyes wander, seeking out the group of young men seated at the bar. They're not a large group, but they're loud and boisterous, with several flights of wine lining the counter like shots.

In my age range.

Several of them gather up their stem less wine glasses, their course of action to head in our direction. I stand taller, assessing.

The leader is a few paces ahead of the rest, his laser-like focus hell bent to reach us first. Undoubtedly so he can control the situation, or have first pick. Or both. I know his type—cocky swagger, lopsided grin meant to be captivating, tight white tee, and straining muscles that can only be obtained with hour-upon-hour at the gym. If that weren't enough, a visible tattoo snakes up the side of his neck and disappears into his hairline. An arrogant grin with blaring white teeth complete the unappealing package.

Wow. This guy thinks he's the shit.

The other three, well they trail along after him like afterthoughts. The 'yes' men, donning the official uniform of "Mr. One-Night Stand:" tight shirts, bleached teeth, and matching shit-eating grins. I bet two out of three of them have rib tats.

Except the straggler.

I eyeball the guy shuffling behind them, my green gaze *fixating* on him, latching on with fascination; not only is he deliberately lagging behind, he looks damn uncomfortable. This one… he's a complete paradox.

Dark, tousled hair, The Straggler effortlessly dons a gingham plaid shirt, neatly tucked under a preppy blue sweater vest, and a belted pair of navy khakis. His only concession to casual: rolled shirt sleeves pushed to his elbows.

All he's missing is a bow tie.

Honestly? The poor guy looks like he's just arrived from the office; a tax attorney's office, I speculate. Or a cubicle at a technology company. Yeah, definitely computer programming.

Or insurance sales.

Wait, no. The internal revenue service.

I bet he's an auditor; that sounds boring.

I'm not trying to be being mean, but the guy is wearing *khakis* and a sweater vest in a bar on a *weekend*, for heaven's sake. He's practically begging me to judge him.

To the upwardly mobile, wearing a plaid shirt to a bar during the workweek would be just fine; but not on a Saturday. Unless of course, he happens to be from the deep south—maybe Georgia or South Carolina? Don't they wear bow ties down there? Yeah. They do.

I study him further and after some serious contemplation, concede that The Straggler pulls off the stuffy look *just* fine.

And did I mention his glasses?

Kind of adorkable.

He pushes those tortoise shell rims up the bridge of a straight nose on an average face, crosses his average arms across an average chest, and I watch as he tips his head towards the ceiling and murmurs to himself.

Adam's apple bobbing, I read his lips: *I'm in hell.*

Nope. I'm not eyeballing the guy because I'm interested; I'm eyeballing him because he's so *obviously* miserable.

Is it sick that I'm enjoying his discomfort? Ugh, what is wrong with me?

Smirking, I bring the bowl of my wineglass to my lips, concealing the smile growing there as the guys approach, confidently, like a pack of vultures. Swallowing a chuckle, I gulp my wine.

"Hey, I think I recognize that guy," Tabitha says, her

eyes squinting at The Straggler, then snapping her fingers. "*Ha*! Yes, I do. I'm pretty sure that's Collin's friend Dex. Dexter Ryan? I think."

Dexter.

I turn the name around inside my head, testing it out.

How nerdy.

But it fits.

And I like it.

One

Daphne

All my friends are falling in love and it sucks.

Don't get me wrong; I love them all and I'm happy for them, but sometimes it would be nice to call them up and have them be readily available. Up for anything, including an impromptu night out.

Or a night in.

These days, it takes days—if not weeks, to coordinate the simplest get together. Why? Because none of my friends can plan something without asking their significant other. "Let me check with Collin…" or "I think we have plans, but let me ask…" or "Collin's coming home that night from his business trip and I want to be here when he gets back…"

If I wasn't so damn happy for my friends, I would feel sorry for myself.

Okay, fine. I *do* feel sorry for myself.

And how will I rectify that? By drowning my self-wallowing emotions in the form of buttery popcorn and movie theater chocolate, of course.

Trust me: it works every time. It's foolproof, if not fleeting, but at the moment, I don't care.

Alone in the lobby, I clutch my movie stub and stand patiently in line at the concession stand, staring up at the glowing menu board, debating between adding butter to my popcorn. Do I want SnowCaps or Bunch of Crunch? Twenty ounces of soda, or thirty?

Unhurriedly, since I'm a good fifteen minutes early, I watch as the teenagers behind the glass counters avoid smashing into each other as they grab treats, food, and fill beverage cups. Ring customers up.

I cringe as a young man with spiky hair drops a cardboard tray of freshly nuked White Castle burgers to the tile floor, his shoulders slumping in dismay at his error.

Poor kid.

Reaching the front of the line, I tap my folded twenty-dollar bill on the glass counter, watching as he quickly fills a new box with the tiny burgers for the guy in the next line over, as a manager swoops in with a broom to sweep up the mess behind him.

Already having mentally placed my order, I absent-mindedly cast a sidelong glance around the concession stand lines, taking in the people. Couple after couple. Small groups of teenagers. Families. Sci-Fi nerds coming to see a re-mastered version of a classic. Customer after customer steps up to the counter to order munchies and drinks, and I'm ready to repeat my order when a lone figure in an expensive blue coat catches my wandering eyes.

I do a double take.

Wait. I think I recognize that guy. Is that…

It is.

Dexter.

Dexter Ryan.

Collin Keller's good friend from the other night.

We hardly spoke that night at Ripley's Wine Bar, but I'm good with faces and would recognize him anywhere. I mean, seriously, who could forget the guy wearing a sweater vest at a bar on a Saturday night?

I watch him now, inwardly cringing.

Fine. *Out*wardly cringing, sinking deeper into my puffer vest; of course I'd bump into someone I knew—even in passing—while I was at the movies alone.

Completely.

Alone.

What were the freaking odds?

Covertly, I watch him from under my long dark lashes, thankful I'm somewhat cleverly disguised in a knit winter hat and non-prescription glasses, and barely distinguishable. At least, I hope so.

Dexter, for his part, looks polished and geeky and smart and oddly kind of…

Sexy.

In a very geeky way.

Ugh.

"Ma'am?"

A voice interrupts my thoughts.

"Ma'am, are you ready to order?" A teenage girl behind the concession counter stares back at me like I'm an oddity. "*Ma'am?*"

Ma'am? Oh shit, she's talking to *me*.

Sporting a bright, azure blue baseball cap with the movie theater logo embroidered on it in white, the girl's black hair sticks out the bottom in a frizzy, messy bun, tips dyed a shocking yellow. Six earrings line her left ear, one of them a hot pink barbell. Her dull gray eyes are rimmed in heavy black kohl, and she regards me impatiently.

Like I'm a mental person.

"Sorry, I thought you were talking to someone else."

Black eyebrows raised, her pointer finger hovers above the cash register buttons, ready to strike.

Rattling off my order—the same order every time I come to the movies—it's not long before another teen behind the booth assists her, dropping a big tub of fluffy, buttery popcorn unceremoniously on the counter.

Each and every kernel for me, and me alone.

Chocolate.

Soda.

As I'm pondering more bad choices, like adding licorice or Swedish Fish, the teenage girl interrupts. "If you order *another* drink for your friend, you get a discount on both beverages of fifty cents. Your total would be $23.11 instead of $24.11"

Her monotone voice offers me the discount deal; her eyes say she doesn't give a shit if I take it.

I give a tight lipped smile, tapping my debit card on the glass counter; no way is a twenty-dollar bill going to cover all this food. "There is no friend. It's just little 'ol me, thanks."

Her eyes troll to the colossal popcorn bucket, chocolate and drink. "It's just *you*?" She damn near shouts. "Sorry, I mean—just the one beverage?"

Could she be any louder? Could we *not* broadcast to

everyone I'm flying solo at the movies?

I nod, affirmative, wishing she'd lower her voice a few decibels. "Yes, just the one beverage. Wait. I'll take a bottle of water, too, please."

Of course, it's my fault she thought I was part of a couple when I ordered the large with extra butter, box of Snowcaps on the side, and a soda.

I pay, trying to scurry undetected to the condiments, putting both my beverages into a cardboard snack tray, awkwardly juggling it as I pluck a few napkins from the metallic holder. One, two... five napkins.

That should be enough, right?

For good measure, I pluck out two more from the holder because sometimes my butter hands get out of control. I hate having buttery fingerprints.

Still clutching my ticket stub, I attempt to lift it to see which theater my movie is playing in, but fail miserably and have to set everyth—

"Daphne?"

I freeze.

Look up.

Pivot.

Standing behind me in his navy blue pea coat, Dexter Ryan smiles crookedly down at me.

He smoothes his hands down the front of his dark pressed jeans—or is he wiping sweat off his palms?—and pushes his tortoiseshell glasses up the bridge of his nose.

I take it all in—every inch of him—from the preppy jacket, the glasses, the slight cleft in his chin, up to the black cable knit winter hat when he suddenly removes it. Instead of his hair being flattened by the hat, it's unruly and a bit tousled. A rich brown, his locks are wavy, shaggy and desperately need a trim.

He finger combs it out of his face.

"It *is* Daphne, right?" He asks, unsure of himself.

It's hard to hold back my groan of dismay at being spotted, but I muster up a cheerful, "Yeah. Hi. Dexter?"

He smiles then, his eyes shining behind his dark, tortoiseshell lenses. I mean—I *think* his eyes are shining. Maybe it's just the reflection of his glasses?

Those dark eyes dart down to my snacks, the ticket stub grasped between two fingers on my right hand. His brows go up. "Do you need help with anything? Sorry, I'm an idiot; it's obvious you're waiting for someone."

A nervous giggle escapes my lips, only I can't smack a hand over my mouth to stop it. "Gosh thank you. I don't need help," I hurriedly say. "I just have to see which theater I'm in, but I'm having a hard time with…"

All my food.

"It's just you?" His head cranes around, confused. "I'm sorry, that was rude. Of course it's not just you. Why would it be?" His deep voice gives a forced, nervous chuckle.

Wow, this is about to get awkward. "Nope, it *is* just me," I barely manage to get the words out. "I'm here alone."

Dexter's eyes go wide, sending his brows straight into his hairline. His mouth even falls open a little but no sound comes out.

"Great," I joke, more for my benefit than his. "I've rendered you speechless."

I follow the line of his jacket, down to the hand tightly gripping his winter hat.

"No! Shit, sorry. I didn't mean… I don't know what I

mean." Deep breath. "I'm here alone, too."

Suddenly, his mouth twitches into a goofy grin, and my green eyes make a beeline to his lips as they form the words, "Which movie are you here to see?"

Those lips.

Huh?

Instead of formulating a response, I find myself trying not to stare at a perfectly sculpted upper lip and a full mouth surrounded by a days' worth of five o'clock shadow. Strong jawline. Straight, white teeth. And is that line in his cheek a dimple?

Dexter clears his throat, and I watch transfixed as the chords in his neck flex when he reprises, "Which movie are you here to see?"

Huh?

"Huh?"

Jesus, I have some serious issues. And if Dexter thinks I've gone space cadet on him, he doesn't let on; his brown eyes are kind. Friendly. Sincere without a trace of egotism. "What movie?"

Oh god. Could this be any more humiliating? The guy's asked me the same question three times.

"Uh... StarGate?"

Don't judge me! *Don't judge me, Dexter!* I want to shout. I want to hide behind my massive bucket of popcorn. *Yes, it's true! I am at a nine o'clock screening of StarGate, the twenty-year-old movie turned nerd cult classic of all time.*

By myself.

As in: alone.

On a Saturday night.

A pleased grin quirks, his thick brows shoot up for a

second time in surprise before he clears his throat. "Me too."

Dexter briefly glances down at his ticket stub, pushing his glasses back up the bridge of his nose with a forefinger. God, it's such a sweet gesture I actually cock my head and stare.

Truth be told, I could probably stare at him all night.

It's been all of three minutes and I find him charming, adorable, and unassumingly handsome. The kind of handsome that sneaks up on you.

He clears his throat again. "It's, uh, in theater twelve. Let me just…" He reaches around me then to grab a few napkins for himself, though he's only carrying a medium soda.

No popcorn. No candy. No snacks.

Wait. *No snacks*?

Who doesn't get *snacks* at the movies? Who?

Self-conscious of my gluttony, I back away, wielding my embarrassing armload of junk food, face flaming hot. "I guess I should go find myself a seat. Yeah. I should go do that. The previews have probably already started and those are my favorite part…"

Stop talking Daphne!

Dexter nods and grapples for a few more napkins.

Oh brother; between the two of us, we have enough napkins to last us through Armageddon.

"Alright, well…" We both move gracelessly at the same time, in the same direction, doing that awkward sidestepping dance you do when you're trying to get around someone, but failing miserably.

"Here, let me at least carry something for you," Dexter offers, reaching to take the beverage tray out of my hands.

"Thank you." I laugh nervously, a horrible hot, furious blush creeping up my neck. "We go this way, I guess."

Walking towards the same hallway, it's obvious neither of us knows what the proper etiquette is when you run into someone at the movie theater when you're flying solo, and seeing the same movie. I'm aware of his every movement; every sidelong glance he surreptitiously gives me along the way.

Without speaking, we lumber down the endless, empty hallway, kernels from my popcorn bucket occasionally falling weightlessly to the carpet below. I look behind me down at the trail; I'm *such* a Gretel.

When we reach theater twelve, Dexter beats me to the door, his arm shooting out to grab the door handle, pulling it open, and waiting for me to walk through first. It's such a gentlemanly thing to do.

Something a date would do, I can't help but muse with longing.

The theater is packed, dark and—dammit, the previews have started! Disappointed, my eyes scan row after occupied row, seeking out in the dim one empty spot—*any* empty spot *not* near the front. I would rather poke my eye out with a stick than sit in the front row, and luckily, I find several halfway up.

I *feel* Dexter hesitate on the steps as he approaches me from behind, just as I sense him internally debating his options; should he say good-bye and go in search of his own seat? Or should he tag along and sit with me, not knowing if he'll be welcome?

How do I know he's thinking this? Easy. Because I'm feeling it, too. Should I invite him to sit next to me?

Would that be awkward? Probably, but wouldn't it be worse knowing he's a few seats behind me, staring at the back of my head?

Slowly, guided by the illuminated track lighting on the stairs, I climb step after step. Ascending to the middle row, eyes seeking—scanning in the dark, until…

There, three rows up, are two seats.

Together.

What were the odds?

Over my shoulder I softly whisper, "Those?"

"Sure."

Together we shimmy our way towards the empty seats, making apologies, sidestepping purses, popcorn buckets, and legs in the dimly lit space.

Once we're seated, settled in, Dexter removes his pea coat, and I watch him unhook each double toggle button from the corner of my eye. His heavy coat comes off and the woodsy, male smell of him reaches my sensitive nose.

Good lord he smells freaking fantastic. Like a fresh shower and fresh air and wintergreen toothpaste.

The truth blindsides me: I'm *insanely* attracted to this guy.

He's such a dork.

But *so*, so cute.

I stuff a handful of popcorn in my mouth to occupy myself—it weighs down my tongue like sandpaper—and when I crunch down, the speakers in the theater choose *that* moment to go dead silent, filling the silence around us with the sound of my chewing.

Mortified, I pause.

Chew.

Pause.

Oh my god, I'm so loud.
Chew.
I give Dexter a weak, popcorn-filled smile before my head falls back on the headrest and I smother a groan by shoving more popcorn in my face.
I hate myself right now.

Dexter

Daphne Winthrop.

The woman I spent half my weekend stalking on social media after meeting her at Ripley's Wine Bar because—let's face it—she is beautiful.

She's also way out of my league.

Outgoing, charismatic and sweet, I try not to watch as she nervously shovels handful after handful of buttered popcorn into her gullet from that giant bucket, and ignore the sidelong glances from her piercing green eyes.

The brightest green eyes I've ever seen in person.

God, she must think I'm a freaking loser.

I mean—coming to a movie alone, on a Saturday night? And StarGate of all things.

Christ.

Why couldn't it have been something cool, like Star Wars or Planet of the Apes?

For a split second I want to lean over and ask Daphne what *she's* doing here alone, but think better of it; she looked mortified when I approached her at the condiments counter, but really—I *did* need those napkins.

In front of us, the movie previews roll on. Holiday, comedy and zombie Coming Attractions quickly flash on the two-story mega screen below but I'm not paying one goddamn bit of attention. Nope. Instead of being riveted on the digital display, my traitorous eyes spend their time stealthily sneaking peeks at Daphne.

They trail her movements when she finally sets the large tub of popcorn on the hard, concrete floor at our feet. They watch as she unzips her puffer vest, shrugging out of it then twisting her body to drape the vest over the back of her seat. Even in the shadowy theater, I notice her breasts strain against the fabric of her fuzzy lavender sweater when she arches her back.

Her breasts, her breasts.

Shit, what am I doing staring at her breasts?

Getting turned on, that's what.

I haven't gotten laid since I broke it off with my ex-girlfriend Charlotte eighteen months ago, and haven't had a real date in over ten months; in case anyone wanted to fact check the math, that's roughly three hundred and four days of missed opportunities. Give or take.

And yes—I counted.

Daphne leaves her gray winter hat on, her long brown hair frames one of the prettiest fucking heart-shaped faces I've ever seen, and shines glossy beneath the changing lights of the big screen.

Black framed glasses she hadn't had on the other night lend a stark contrast to the sexy, confident Daphne who was out with her friends at Ripley's Wine Bar. Don't get me wrong; she was nice enough—but that Daphne wouldn't ordinarily give me the time of day.

This Daphne… she's better.

Casual. *Soft*. Approachable.

Plus, she came to fucking StarGate alone on a Saturday night. Who does that?

I mean—besides nerds like me.

Not beautiful girls like Daphne, with full social calendars. Girls with *great* bodies and better personalities. Fun loving. Girls who have guys lined up for their phone numbers—and I would know, because I saw it with my own eyes last weekend.

I give her another curious glance, wondering why someone like her isn't on a date tonight. Me? That one is easy: I'm perpetually put in the Friend Zone because I'm *nice*. Easy going. A commitment kind of guy that doesn't take the time to date around, I'm more likely to be found chaperoning my kid sisters school dance than asking someone on a date.

So, I get why *I'm* here alone—but why is she?

Her head turns and our eyes meet when she bends to grab her popcorn bucket off the floor. In the dark, I see her mouth curve into a friendly smile; Daphne's eyes rest on me a few steady heartbeats before she turns her attention back to the movie screen. Her hand digs in the giant tub of popcorn like she's rooting around for buried treasure.

She pops a kernel in her open mouth.

Chews.

Swallows.

"Want some?" She offers in a whisper, holding the tub between us.

I don't—but I'm also smart enough to know that when a pretty girl offers you something—*you take it*. "Sure, thanks."

She beams at me in the dark. A friendly, *platonic* smile.

Platonic: story of my life.

THINGS LIARS FAKE

However, I'm not complaining twenty-minutes later when Daphne is frantically seizing my upper arm as an enemy ship onscreen (an enemy of Planet Dakara) launches an attack against Colonel O'Neil. In the distance, explosives go off, and a spacecraft is blasted into smithereens.

It's loud, bloody, and pretty fucking intense.

Daphne gasps when someone onscreen is violently shot, her fingers wrapping tighter around my bicep. Another blast and she buries her face in the shoulder of my plaid, flannel shirt.

A tad melodramatic?

Yes.

Do I give a shit?

Hell no.

Without hesitating, my neck dips down and I inhale, giving her a quick whiff. She smells like heaven; I mean, if heaven smelt like butter and chocolate.

"Can I look now?" Comes her muffled voice. She peeks up at the screen with one eye. "Is it safe to come out?"

"Yeah, it's safe," my chest rumbles with laughter.

Daphne sits up then, still holding my forearm.

"Sorry about that. Sometimes I get a little…" Her hand unnecessarily presses down the sleeve of my shirt to smooth out wrinkles that don't exist, and then—is it my imagination, or are her fingers running the length of my forearm? I swear she just gave it a squeeze.

Biting her lower lip, she shoots me an innocent smile in the dark, causing my heart to do some weird shit inside my chest.

Not to mention the stirring of *other things* in my pants.

If I was a girl, I might sigh.
Daphne Winthrop may just be the girl of my dreams.

Two

Daphne

Not going to lie: I barely saw *a single minute* of that movie.

Why?

Obviously I was distracted by Dexter.

Judging by the way he sniffed my hat when I had my head buried in his shoulder, I suspect he didn't see much of the movie, either.

In fact, I suspect a great *many* things about Dexter: such as his need for punctuality. He *looks* like he's always on time. I know you shouldn't judge a book by its cover, but his wearing a sweater vest and dress shirt to the bar last weekend lends me to believe he's no stranger to buttoned up and slightly stuffy.

I suspect he thrives on structure and order.

I suspect he probably takes life a bit *too* seriously.

A little too lanky, a little too quiet, and tad too aloof, he's hardly the kind of guy a girl writes home about. Dexter is definitely not the kind of guy that inspires fantasies in a young woman—sexual or otherwise.

And yet...

When the credits roll at the end, we stay seated, watching name after name scroll across the giant screen down in front. I turn my head towards Dexter and ask, "What'd you think about the part when they found the interstellar teleportation device?"

I'm such a nerd sometimes.

"Uh, hello. Not gonna lie; I kind of *want* one of those now and I'm not ashamed to admit it," he says as the wall sconces in the room illuminate the cavernous room, the people around us rising and heading towards the exits.

"We could battle if we both had light sabers."

"That's Stars Wars," he points out.

"So?"

"You can't mix Universes," He says in a *duh* kind of tone. Like I should know better.

I let out a long, dramatic sigh. "True. But you're probably just saying that because you don't want me to Princess Leia your ass. I would *destroy* you."

Dexter laughs, tipping his head back against the cushioned seat. "Are you shitting me? I'd *pay* to see you dressed as Princess Leia."

My eyes must get wide because he clamps his lips shut and looks away, embarrassed.

We sit in compatible silence a few seconds before I break it. "Isn't it crazy how twenty years ago, the technology in this movie was cutting edge?"

This perks him up. "Right? Imagine how incredible the movie would be if they remade it."

"I was thinking the same thing!"

"Don't judge me, but I have a small army of Star Wars Storm Troopers on my desktop at work. My sisters gave them to me for Christmas a few years ago. They look so bad ass on my computer."

I sit up straighter in my seat, interested. "Where do you work?"

"I'm in wealth management at a firm downtown. Right on Michigan Avenue. What about you?" Dexter asks as he removes the plastic lid from his soda, shakes the ice around, and tips his head back for a drink. A small bead of liquid glistens, wet, on his bottom lip, and I stare.

Oblivious to my ogling, he licks it off, daring my eyes not to follow the movement of his tongue.

"Daphne?" He waves a hand in front of my face. "Hello?"

"I'm sorry, you were asking where I work?"

He replaces the lid on his soda and laughs around the straw. "Yeah, where do you work?"

What I want to say is, "At the corner of *Get Inside My Pants and Let's Make Out...*" but what I *actually say* is: "I'm about ten minutes from here, at a boutique PR firm; Dorser & Kohl Marketing. I've been with them since I graduated and absolutely love it."

God, I am so boring.

We stare at each other then, two matching stupid grins on our faces. Dexter's smile gets wider when my teeth bite down on my bottom lip to stop the nervous giggle bubbling up from inside me.

Just then, overhead lights flood the theater, and a teenage crew comes in to clean, bustling in loudly with brooms and dustpans. One teenager noisily drags a garbage can behind him, so Dexter and I have no choice but to grudgingly remove our butts from the cushiony theater chairs and rise to our feet, collect our jackets and garbage, and make towards the exit.

Well, mostly *my* garbage since I was the only one stuffing my face with snacks.

"This was fun," he says as we trudge down the bright hallway, into the crowded lobby. "I'm glad I ran into you."

I feel my face heat. "Yeah, me too." I pause in front of the bathroom, gesturing. "Would you mind waiting? I have to…"

Pee.

"Here, let me hold these for you." Dexter takes the tub of popcorn out of my hands, my water bottle, purse, and candy wrappers. "Do you wanna toss any of this in the trash?"

He is *so* sweet and nice.

"Sure. If you don't mind. Wait! Maybe keep the popcorn?"

I'll munch on that in the car.

A few minutes later, I'm washing my hands and rejoining Dexter, who holds my puffer vest out and open to assist me into it, and I pivot so I can slide my arms through the holes.

Sweet and nice and a *gentleman.*

A trifecta.

"This was fun," he repeats when I turn to face him. I look him up and down, watching as he slips into his heavy wool coat. His shoulders might not be wide and athletic, but I can tell they're lean and fit. I watch, riveted, as his masculine fingers deftly work the toggle buttons. They're long, strong, and male.

Unexpectedly, in my mind, I'm picturing them running slowly under the hem of my sweater, over my bare stomach, and up my—

Crap. And here I thought Tabitha was the one with a vivid, sexy imagination. Or maybe I need to go reread her sexy romance novel. Again. For the fifth time.

Glancing away, I try to keep my dirty thoughts at bay. I mean, *Jesus*! What the hell am I *doing*, goggling the poor guy's hands like they're sexual objects?

If only he knew.

Raising my hands to my cheeks, I find them flaming hot: a common theme tonight.

My eyes continue tracking his movements; he pulls the winter hat out of his pocket, drawing it down over his mop of hair. His nose twitches, shifting his glasses into place; a move I find incredibly adorable, if not a tad dorky.

Swallowing hard, I smile. "It really was fun. It was nice having company for a change. I usually…" I draw in a breath. "Normally I come watch these old Sci-Fi movies, um. Alone."

Dexter shifts his feet, and I look down at the brown dress shoes more suited for the office than a casual night at the cinema.

"Uh, so." Dexter takes a deep breath, stuffing his hands into the pockets of his coat. Exhales out. "So maybe…" He pauses to push up those tortoiseshell frames with the tip of his finger.

This is it. He's going to ask me on a date.

I lean towards him, bucket of popcorn tipping, anticipation making my body hum. "Yes?"

Does my voice sound breathy? Over eager? Shoot. Cool it Daphne; bring the desperation down a notch.

Dexter hesitates, rocking back on his heels. "So maybe—"

"Dex, sweetie, is that *you*?" A shrill female voice interrupts his entreaty, causing us both to twist around, surprised at the woman approaching us at a hastened pace. Short with sandy blonde hair, the woman looks around my mother's age and is sporting a wide, toothy grin. "I thought that was you! What a pleasant surprise."

She envelopes him in a full contact hug, her arms squeezing.

"Aunt Bethany." He sounds pained when she finally peels herself away. "I'm surprised to see you. Who are you here with so late?"

"Late?" She laughs, loud and tinkly, and checks her watch. "It's only eleven forty-five on a Saturday night! I'm old but not *that* old." Aunt Bethany's eyebrows raise when focusing her attention on me, intense gaze alive.

Mischievous.

Her pink lips form an 'O' of glee.

"I don't mean to intrude on your *date*. I just wanted to come over and say hello." Aunt Bethany scrutinizes me with wide, interested brown eyes; not in a negative way. No. Quite the opposite—she's so excited she almost looks euphoric. Ready to burst. "Dexter sweetie, are you going to introduce me to your *friend*?"

She says the word friend innocuously enough, but what she really means is: *friend*-friend. As in: girlfriend.

Dexter sticks his hands back into the pockets of his thick coat. "Aunt B, this is my friend Daphne. Daphne, this is my mom's youngest sister. My Aunt B."

Bethany wastes no time extending her open arms towards me and pulling me in for a hug, which is super awkward since I'm still clutching my popcorn. Her embrace pins my arms to the side before she squeezes the life out of me, thereby crushing my bucket.

I'm positive a few kernels fall to the ground.

"So good to meet you," I croak into her curly hair, gasping for air. Sneaking a glance over her shoulder at Dexter's stricken face, I try desperately not to laugh.

I fail.

Aunt B gives me one more squeeze before releasing me, then steps back to look me up and down with a sigh. "You are gorgeous. Those green eyes are stunning. Dex, she's gorgeous."

Dexter blushes furiously, removing a hand from his pocket to adjust his glasses while his Aunt continues fussing, oblivious to his obvious discomfort.

"Where has he been *hiding* you! Never mind, don't answer that; it's none of my business. The real question is, are you bringing her to Grace's engagement party next weekend? Wait, don't answer that!"

I don't want to embarrass Dexter further by reminding his Aunt we're just friends; one's who have only met twice—not that the first time at Ripley's Wine Bar counts since we hardly spoke.

So instead, I go with, "Um."

"Has his *mother* met you yet?" Bethany asks, eyes sparkling. She is completely giddy.

I cast a helpless look at Dexter; he shakes his head, so I answer truthfully. "No ma'am."

"No ma'am." She parrots. "*Ugh*, I love that. You sound positively southern. Say something else. Say *y'all*."

Laughing, I fake a southern accent (which I happen to be really good at) for his eccentric Aunt, whom I'll never see again in my life. I put a hand on my hip for added effect and wave my other hand about airily.

"How y'all doin'? When life hands you lemons, put them in your sweet tea and thank Gawd you're from the South." I fan myself, channeling my inner Scarlet O'Hara and getting into the role. "*Fiddle dee-dee!*"

Beside me, Dexter groans, throwing his head back and staring at the ceiling. *Oh my God*, he mouths toward Heaven, running a hand down his face. "Please don't encourage her."

My eyes fly to the cords of his lean neck. His jawline. His Adam's apple. I remove them swiftly when Aunt B follows my line of vision. A knowing smirk crosses her lips.

Crap.

Busted.

His aunt titters gleefully, speaking to her nephew. "Wait until I rub it in your mother's face that I met your girlfriend before she did! She's going to have a cow from the jealously. A *cow*."

"Aunt Bethany, we're not dating. Daphne is *not* my girlfriend." The look he shoots me is apologetic. "Sorry Daphne, I didn't mean to say it like that."

Another blush warms my cheeks.

Bethany brushes him off. "*Ach*, you kids today and your secrecy. Why hide it? Why are you all so afraid of commitment? Please don't tell me you're on The Tinder? That's a trolling site for hook-ups and, you know."

She clucks her tongue, lecturing us on the downsides of dating in the 21st Century. "All you kids do is put everything on-the-line, but you don't want to commit to a relationship."

We *must* look horrified, because she takes one look at us and busts out laughing.

"Fine, fine, I won't say anything if you're trying to keep it a secret. Shhhh, my lips are sealed." She makes another shushing sound, those brown eyes fixated on me. "I don't know if Dex *told* you, but our family tree is full of nuts. I don't blame him for keeping you a secret. Once the family finds out, it's Good night Eileen."

Good night, Eileen? I'm not… What the hell does that even mean?

She jabbers on. "Anywho, I better get going; my friend Brenda ran to the bathroom and she'll have a hissy fit if I'm not standing where she left me when she walks out. Goodness, I can't wait to tell Little Erik I bumped into you."

Dexter snorts and turns to me with a grin. "*Little* Erik is my younger cousin. He kind of idolizes me," he bashfully informs me. "He's named after my Uncle Erik—Big Erik and Little Erik, get it? He's also over six feet tall."

"We like the irony of calling him *little*," Bethany snickers. "It's my favorite joke. Everyone is always expecting a toddler. My poor Sadie inherited all the short genes." She gives her theater soda a shake, back and forth, swirling around the ice inside the cup.

"Sadie is your daughter?" I inquire politely, but genuinely interested.

His Aunt chatters on with great enthusiasm. "Yes! Nineteen going on forty-five; she'd rather stay home and *read* than go out with her friends. You'll meet her at Grace's party if she comes home from school that weekend."

"Aunt B—"

"Oh, don't worry, I'm not gonna tell a soul. Just pretend you never bumped into me." She leans in close, like we're conspiring. "Can you just give me a little nibble of the details though? Where did you two meet? One of those dating sites? MySpace?"

"MySpace isn't a thing anymore, Aunt B."

"Oh. Bumble App?"

Dexter shakes his head. "How do you know about—you know what? Forget I asked."

His composed exterior fading, I put my hand on his forearm to calm him, and he glances down at it before looking into my eyes.

"It's fine," I intone to him quietly. To Bethany I say, "Aunt B, while we're *not* a couple, Dexter and I did meet last weekend when we were both out with friends."

"I was out with Elliot's friends." He supplies reluctantly. "Elliot is a cousin."

Aunt Bethany scrunches up her face. "Elliot? Is he single again? I thought he was dating Kara."

"Nope. Single."

"Good. Kara can do better."

Dexter chuckles, a smile finally tipping his lips. "Yeah, that's probably true."

"Well," Aunt B sighs. "Like I said, I better run." She gives me a once over, eyes shining. "Hold on tight to this one, young lady. He's a keeper."

THINGS LIARS FAKE

Daphne: *You're never going to believe who I ran into at the movie last night.*

Tabitha: *Hold up. First tell me who you went to the movies with, and what did you see?*

Daphne: *StarGate. And I went alone, but that's not my point.*

Tabitha: *You went to another movie alone? I told you to call if you did that! I would have met you there. No man left behind and all that.*

Daphne: *You were on a date. Plus, I repeat: it was Stargate—you hate SciFi.*

Tabitha: *Like that matters. I hate when you go to the movies alone. Plus, I would have sacrificed Collin. He loves that crap.*

Daphne: *I do love you for that offer <3 Anyway... the news is that I ran into Dexter Ryan. He was alone, too, so.... (dot dot dot)*

Tabitha: *Shut. Up. He is such a dork.*

Daphne: *Don't call him a dork! He's really sweet and he saved me from myself. And my giant bucket of popcorn.*

Tabitha: *What is it with you and popcorn? I can never figure it out...*

Daphne: *It's delicious.*

Tabitha: *Alright, so you saw Dexter. I take it you sat with him? Was he as dull as he looks? He's nice and all, but kind of boring, don't you think?*

Daphne: *No. He wasn't dull. He was sweet and adorkable.*

Tabitha: *You know, I should write a book about a hot nerd with a dirty mouth and a hot bod. Would you read it?*
Daphne: *Shut. Up.*
Daphne: *And yes. Yes I would read it...*

Three

Dexter

"Halyard Capitol Investments and Securities, Dexter Ryan speaking." My brisk voice is clear, crisp, and to the point.

"Dexter Ryan, why are you answering your own phone?" My mother's demand shouts at me from the other end of the line. "Where's your secretary?"

For some reason, my mom loves boasting the fact that my firm appointed me my own secretary. Drives me crazy.

I sigh, swiveling in my desk chair towards the window and stare outside at the pond. "She's at lunch, Mom. Occasionally I unchain her from the desk so she can eat."

"I'm going to ignore your sarcasm young man, because I know you're at work and don't have time for a lecture."

I know there's a reason she's calling…

"Who's Daphne?"

And there is.

"She's a friend."

Just a friend; a beautiful, vibrant, and funny friend.

"That's not what your Aunt Bethany said. She said you had a *girl*friend. Why haven't we met her yet? Quite frankly, when she told us she ran into you, my feelings were hurt."

Another thing my mother loves? Guilt trips.

"Your feelings were hurt? Come on, Mom. Bethany was totally over exaggerating to get a rise out of you." I pick up a pencil and start doodling circles on a notepad. "Wait. Who's this *we*? What *we* are you talking about? Who did Aunt B tell?"

My mom hesitates a heartbeat, then drives home the kill. "Your sisters and I, Aunt Donna and Aunt Tory. We all happened to be together when B called."

The Gossip Network of Ryan Women: once those five catch a whiff of chatter, you might as well rent a billboard in Times Square to broadcast your secrets.

Fuck.

Exasperated, I run a hand through my hair, tugging at the thick strands and releasing a loud puff of air. I can feel the ends sticking up in several places, but I'll worry about that later.

"Mom. I'm sorry you're upset, but I'm telling the truth. Daphne is just my friend. In fact—we've only met twice. I don't know what B told you, but we're not dating."

My mom makes a sniveling sound, and I know she's digging deep for a tear. "Dexter Phillip, don't lie to me. It hurts my feelings."

I lean back in my desk chair, balancing on the back wheels, and stare up at the ceiling. Breathe in and out. "Mom, what reason would I have to lie?"

Another sniffling sound, followed by a scoff. "You tell me."

Drama, drama, drama.

"I—"

"B tells us you're bringing her to Grace's engagement party; she was *rather* pleased to rub the news in. You know I hate when she finds things out first; and about my own son?"

"Mom—"

"It would have been nice if I'd meet your girlfriend first, don't you think?"

Resigned, another long puff of air leaves my throat, and I blow it out into the receiver. "Technically, yeah."

"Bethany said she's just stunning. A petite thing with the sweetest little Southern accent."

A Southern accent? *Jesus Christ.*

My mom continues. "I'm not pleased you kept this from us and I had to find out from B, but Daphne *does* sound lovely."

"She is," slips out before I can stop myself.

Mom sighs one of those wistful, breathless sighs woman breathe when they're overcome with joy. I roll my eyes and watch as the landscapers outside walk back-and-forth across the parking lot with leaf blowers. Another drives a riding lawn mower so fast through the grass it's like he's vying to race Danica Patrick's NASCAR.

Grass flies everywhere.

"Come a little early, please, so she can meet us before we head into the party. I won't get the chance to talk to her when we're there. Gracie's invited over a hundred people. Tory told me it's turned into quite the circus."

My cousin Grace has always been high-maintenance, so this news doesn't surprise me in the least. Her brother, Elliot, is the dickhead who stood me up at the Wine Bar last weekend.

"Come early? Uh… that might be hard to swing. I'm pulling extra hours next Saturday."

Mom sighs loudly, long-suffering.

"Just make sure you tell her it's formal. I assume you're wearing a suit?"

Silence.

"Dexter, are you listening?"

I glance down at the Blue Chip stock portfolios stacked on my desk. The three million plus dollar contract, open to its annual shareholder's report, sits atop another one point five-million-dollar portfolio I manage.

Millions of dollars, dividends, and reserves; all whose investment future earnings rest in *my* capable hands while my *mother* lectures me on the phone about a girlfriend I don't even have.

This irony is not lost on me.

"Yes, I'm listening."

"Formal attire." Pause. "And Dexter?"

"Yeah?" The pen in my hand stops drawing circles, and I flick it across the desk. It hits the hard surface of the wall, ricochets then falls off the far edge with a satisfying clatter.

"We're happy for you honey."

I can only grunt out a reply.

THINGS LIARS FAKE

This is ridiculous.

I've been staring at my phone for the better half of an hour, debating my options about whether or not to call Daphne.

I mean, other than the fact that this is a horrible fucking idea, why not pick up the phone and call?

So:

I hunt her number down online and call her at work to propose this ridiculous scheme.

Or.

I can *not* call Daphne, inventing an elaborate explanation for her absence to appease my meddlesome family.

Or.

I can do the honorable thing and show up to the engagement party alone; tell everyone the truth. There would be no shame in that, simple misunderstanding that it was.

But if I'm being honest…

I want to see her again.

Not gonna lie.

Fucked up as it sounds, I'm willing to concoct an elaborate charade and look like an ass just to see her again.

I think about my mom and my sisters, then my dickhead cousin Elliot, whose guaran-goddamn-tee'd to have his ex-girlfriend Kara at the party hanging all over him, even though he's broken up with her a few times.

See, Elliot subscribes to the motto *man-kind isn't meant for monogamy*. His past girlfriends, historically, eventually find issue with this motto, and once they do—they typically begin the process of trying to change him (ie. get him to be faithful). Immediately getting themselves dumped.

Elliot has dumped Kara twice, once at a family function, and once before Valentine's Day just so he wouldn't have to pay for a fancy dinner on the 14th.

They got back together on the 15th.

Kara, who has huge surgically enhanced tits, bleach blonde hair, and applies her make up with a painter's palette knife. Kara, who has the IQ of a plastic Barbie doll—maybe even lower. Kara, who giggles like an eight-year-old. My point is: Elliot thinks he's *hot shit* because he's dating a woman that looks like a Playboy centerfold.

Kara's elevator might not go all the way to the top floor, but Elliot thinks she's smoking hot and his opinion is the only one that counts.

I guess I'd feel like hot shit too if I liked parading around cheap looking woman.

Which I do not.

My last girlfriend, Charlotte, was a paralegal at a law firm whose offices occupy the top floor in our building. Classy and serious, we both ultimately wanted the same things out a relationship—marriage, kids, and a house outside of the city.

But there was always something missing; something exciting.

Everything with Char was… *fine*. Predictable.
Vanilla.
Boring?
Missionary sex, buttoned-up cardigan sweaters—even on the weekends—unless she was wearing her Northwestern sweatshirt to do her gardening. Yawn.

Char was cute, if not a little… plain. Straight brown

bob trimmed exactly every six weeks, serious brown eyes, she reserved her mega-watt smiles for the partners in her law firm, her close friends, and occasionally—me.

Bottom line: the sight of her entering a room didn't get my dick hard.

The staid climate of our relationship wasn't doing it for me anymore. There was never any anticipation. Never any spontaneity.

Never any fun.

Sure, I've been on a few dates since breaking it off with Charlotte; with more quiet, serious girls. Girls who sipped wine and stopped at one glass. Girls who counted networking as a hobby, drank three double shot Starbucks a day so they could work late, and gave tight smiles instead of laughing.

Fucking depressing.

And for whatever reason, my asshole cousin finds it *hilarious* to bring up my relationship status at every opportunity. No idea why. Like having a date is supposed to define my character. Like having a date makes me more masculine.

Honestly, I'd rather be completely alone and a decent guy, than a douchebag with a shitty date.

Elliot is a dickhole.

My thoughts stray to Daphne, her long silky hair and green eyes. The black framed glasses. Her glossy pink lips tipped up into a sly smile. Her sexy, easy, musical laugh.

I palm the computer mouse, scrolling it around its pad, waiting for my Dundler Mifflin screensaver to disappear, and pull up Google.

Type in Dorser & Kohl Marketing.

The firm's website pops up in the search results, and I

click on the link, scrolling through the site for employee profiles until I find hers.

Daphne Winthrop: Junior Vice President of Public Relations.

Buttoned to the collar in a blouse, she's leaning against a stone building, arms crossed. Black blazer and pressed slacks, profile shot is classy, conservative and professional.

I read her bio; Age, 26. Graduated from State with a BA in Business. Alum of two professional fraternity organizations. Volunteer coordinator for a women's shelter. Hobbies: travel, skiing and reading.

It says nothing about StarGate, alternative Universes, or fangirling over vintage Sci-Fi movies. In fact, everything about her bio reads as 'my usual type.'

Exactly my type.

Only I know differently.

My hand hovers over the mouse, and I scroll until I find her contact information. Eight seconds later I'm staring, in color, at her phone number. Should I call? Text? Or send an email?

What the hell am I going to say? *Hi Daphne, this is Dexter Ryan. Remember me from last night? I'm going to need you at that engagement party my aunt was yammering on-and-on about. Turns out my family is riding my ass. They're driving me crazy, and you'd be doing me a huge favor if you pretended to be my girlfriend for an evening…*

Right; because that doesn't sound fucked up.

And yet, I don't abandon the idea entirely—not with my buddy Collin running around in my head shouting 'Balls to the wall, Dex. Balls to the fucking walls!' Collin, who pursued his girlfriend relentlessly, and who doesn't give a shit what people think of him.

He'd call her without hesitating and expect me to do the same. Shit, he'd dial the phone for me.

But unlike Collin's girlfriend Tabitha, *this* gorgeous girl is not going to want me to call her.

No way.

I palm the phone in my hand and push the glasses up the bridge of my nose, leaning back in my desk chair and swiveling it around a few times before setting the phone back down. My computer pings with an email notification and I rotate my chair back towards the desktop, click open the message, scanning it absentmindedly.

Noting that it's just a follow up on an account I just picked up from a competitor's firm, I flag it as priority, but close the window.

I can't focus.

Frustrated, I raise both hands and run my fingers through my thick brown hair, shake my head and let out a loud groan.

"Dammit!" I curse loudly.

Loud enough that my secretary Vanessa sticks her head in my office door.

Shit.

"Is everything okay in here, Sir?" Worry is etched across her face, but that's nothing new. A few weeks ago, Vanessa fucked up some client files and almost lost us a major account; these days her paranoia with the risk of being fired is at an all-time high—despite my constant reassurances that her job is secure.

For the moment, anyway.

"No. Sorry about that. Everything is fine."

Vanessa stands idly for a few seconds, her heavily

mascaraed lashes sticking together briefly as she blinks rapidly at me from the doorway. Tapping the steel doorframe with the palm her hand, so nods slowly. "Sir, do you need anything while I'm up?"

My lips compress in a thin line; I hate when she calls me Sir. It makes me feel like an old man. "Nope. I'm good."

Her coal rimmed eyes narrow. "Alright, if you say so…"

Grabbing my phone, I click open the NEW MESSAGE tab and hit COMPOSE. Then I stare at the small screen, thumbs hovering above the touch screen keypad far too long.

Me: *Daphne, this is Dexter. This might seem really random, but I was hoping you'd be available this week at some point for a quick lunch or coffee?*

Before second-guessing myself, I hit SEND, tap out more messages to random co-workers, switch the ringer to 'vibrate,' and push the phone to the corner of my desk in an attempt to forget about it. It lays there, unmoving for the next six minutes.

I flip it over to check the display screen.

Nothing.

Three seconds later, I check it again.

Still nothing.

This is ridiculous—what the hell am I doing? Not only is this sudden onslaught of nerves uncharacteristic, I have shit tons of work to do with little time to waste. Stacks of paperwork with *millions* of dollars at stake, and here I sit, staring at my goddamn cell phone as if I'm expecting it to sprout wings and fly.

Frustrated by my own insecurities, I pull the top drawer of my desk open and toss the phone in, slamming it shut with resounding bang.

Another four minutes go by and I've accomplished nothing but listening in the silence for my phone's telltale rumble.

Another three, and I've manage to wad up eight pieces of printer paper and basketball toss them to the corner trash can.

Five of them land on the carpet.

I'm about to stand and toss them in the garbage when a low buzzing inside the drawer halts my actions, the vibrating sends my phone thumping spastically inside the hollow wooden interior.

Dammit. I forgot to silence it.

My pulse accelerates.

I lean back in my desk chair, looking into the hall for Vanessa, paranoid— like I'm about to do something criminal and don't want to get caught—before pulling the drawer open and retrieving my sleek phone.

One new message.

It's her.

A bead of sweat actually forms on my brow, and I wipe it with the sleeve of my white dress shirt before swiping open the message center.

Daphne: *Will today work?*

My eyes damn near bug out of my skull. Today?
She wants to meet *today*?
I recall a lecture given to me by my twin, fifteen-year

old sisters about the hazards of responding to a text message immediately: *you just, like, don't do it unless you're a loser*.

I disregard their instructions.

It's stupid advice.

Me: *Yeah, today is great. What time and place work best for you?*

Her reply, too, is almost immediate.

I grin stupidly.

Daphne: *I can probably cut out of work early and bring some things home. So how does two o'clock sound? Do you know where Blooming Grounds is?*

Blooming Grounds is the coffee shop where my childhood friend, Collin, and his girlfriend Tabitha, first began their relationship. It also happens to be less than a block from the offices of Halyard Capitol Investments & Securities.

It will take me five minutes to walk there.

Me: *Two works fine. I will see you at Blooming Grounds.*
Me: *Wait. What can I have waiting for you when you get there?*
Daphne: *How about an iced latte and a blueberry scone?*
Me: *Will do. See you at 2*
Daphne: *LOL*

I stare at that last message from Daphne: LOL.

LOL?

What the hell is that supposed to mean? Is she laughing at something I said? Does she not want me to meet her at two? How the hell am I supposed to interpret *L-O-freaking-L*?

Shit.

I'm twenty-six fucking years old and I need a goddamn girl translator. A nervous knot forms in my stomach; she's either going to laugh in my face when she hears my proposal and tell me to fuck off, or...

I don't even want to think about the alternative.

Four

Daphne

I can't stop watching the clock and counting down the minutes.

One o'clock.

One fifteen.

One twenty-three.

At one forty-five, I shut down my computer. Gathering my belongings, I stuff them in the leather tote I use as a briefcase, and head out to meet Dexter.

There's a carefree little spring in my step as I walk out to my car—a pep that only intensifies with my heart beat when I make the quick drive to the coffee shop, sliding into a tight little parallel parking spot like a champ.

Nervously, I run a hand over my hair, smoothing down the fly-aways. Staring at my reflection in the mirrored sun visor, I wonder what it is about me that had Dexter hesitating to ask me out after the movie—I don't usually get push back from men when I want them to take me out; quite the opposite in fact.

I snap the mirrored sun visor down and grab my purse—a few brisk steps later I'm stepping through the door of Blooming Grounds. The funky interior assails my senses as I take in the eclectic vibe; miss-matched couches line the walls, large green velvet wing back chairs flank the fireplace that's the focal point of the room, and small intimate tables take up the rest of the space.

It's warm. Cozy.

I brush a few tendrils of my long, brown hair out of my face; it's pulled back in a loose chignon, an old-fashioned style that's messy yet sophisticated. Classy yet fun. It looks a whole hell of a lot more complicated than it actually is, and looks amazing.

I pat the back of it confidently letting my green eyes scan the coffee shop, easily finding Dexter seated at a sofa in the corner. Our eyes connect.

He rises.

I take him in from head to toe; a starched, white button down shirt is tucked into slate gray slacks, a slim blue/black and white necktie falling crisply to his waistline. He rakes a hand down that silk tie before adjusting a pair of black glasses; a move I've come to recognize as a nervous habit.

His lips tip into a crooked smile at my approach, and I weave through empty tables towards him.

"Hi," comes my breathless salutation.

"Thanks for coming." Dexter shoves both his hands in the pockets of his pants, then removes them—fidgeting as if he doesn't quite know what to do with himself. I find a spot on the sofa and sit, resting my purse on the worn, patchwork cushions.

Comfy.

He sits in the overstuffed chair across from me, spreading his legs wide and leaning forward with his elbows resting on his knees. He steeples his fingertips.

I try *not* to look between his legs—I really, *really* do—but I'm not gonna lie to you; I sneak a covert peek at his crotch, my face engulfed in flames when my eyes land on the outline of his... junk.

Holy shit, I can actually *see* it through the fabric of his pleated, conservative dress pants; the telltale bulge of his... *Oh my god.*

I am the absolute worst.

The. Worst.

A horrible, perverted human being.

Yup, it's official: Tabitha isn't the only one with a dirty mind.

Although... I am a single, warm-blooded female—one that likes guys and relationships and sex. Definitely sex.

Shooting Dexter a guilty smile, I busy myself, taking large sips from the straw in my latte, mentally chastising myself for having such a depraved mind.

I give the ice in my plastic cup a shake, unable to look him in the eye.

Poor guy doesn't have a clue.

"I'm just going to put this out there to save us time." Dexter takes a deep breath, and exhales. "I told my mom that you'd be at my cousin Grace's engagement party."

Before I can respond, he continues. "You met my Aunt Bethany—did she look like someone who was going to keep our little meeting at the theater a secret? No. The first thing she did from her car in the parking lot was call my mom, who was with my sisters and aunts. So. Yeah."

When he rakes his fingers through his hair, the ends stick up haphazardly.

"Normally I wouldn't commit you to something like that—I mean, we just met and who am I, right? A virtual stranger. Not someone you'd want to spend your weekend with, I get that."

My mouth opens to disagree, but he interrupts.

"I have this cousin Elliot who is a complete douche." My eyebrows go up—not from the word douche; but from *his* use of it. Dexter looks too clean cut and proper to be hurling out vulgarities. "It's getting really fucking old. When my mom called and put me on the spot, I didn't tell her no. So there you have it. I'm in something of a bind, and you're the only one who can help me out of it."

He unsteeples his hands, clasping them instead. "What do you say? Can you stand to spend the night with me as my fake date?"

Wait. Did Dexter just ask me out on a date? My heart skips a beat and I grin so hard my cheeks begin to ache.

"A date?"

Date? Date!

Oh!

"A fake date," he clarifies.

Oh.

"A *fake* date." I repeat.

"Precisely." He nods definitively. "Totally fake. Just drinks, dinner, and if I know my cousin Grace, probably some dancing—but nothing romantic on my end." His hands go up in surrender with a chuckle. "Promise."

Something inside of me deflates. That flare of excitement distinguishes.

I muster up a weak smile.

Oblivious, Dexter grins. "If you could just do me this *one* favor, it would be huge. I would owe you a favor. Maybe even manage your retirement account," he laughs again. "I could probably double your savings in under seven years."

He peers at me hopefully. Naively.

What idiots.

Him. Me. Both of us.

"So? What do you think?"

What do I think? What do I *think*?

I think it's a horrible, stupid, insulting idea. I'm hurt. Pissed. Confused.

So utterly disappointed.

I want to smack him.

He watches me expectantly, his eyes detailing the play of emotions across my face, pushing those black framed glasses up the bridge of his nose.

He looks so… pleased with his idea that my shoulders sag and I feel myself breaking down and giving in.

God, I'm such a sucker.

I make a show of checking the calendar on my phone, poke randomly at the keypad on my phone, and paste a *fake* grin on my face before announcing, "I don't have anything going on this weekend, so yeah. That would work."

He leans forward. "Really?"

"Sure. I'll do it." My brows furrow at his reaction. "Why do you look so surprised?"

The glasses get pushed up again. "I just assumed a girl like you would have plans. A date maybe."

"Like a *real* date as opposed to this *fake* one?" The dig makes those big, chocolate brown eyes widen, so I shrug it off with a joke. "Naw, unless you count me rooted to my couch Netflix and Chilling with my bad self." I recline back on the sofa and cross my legs. "Okay, we're doing this. So what's the plan?"

Five

Dexter

My palms are sweating.

I glance over at Daphne in the passenger seat of my silver Audi, her eyes scanning the landscape as we roll past; houses and businesses becoming further and further apart as I navigate my way out of the city. The long column of her graceful neck is illuminated by the dim glow of street lights.

It's on the cooler side this evening, but Daphne's creamy shoulders are bare beneath a simple, baby blue halter-top thing with a pearl neckline. Tucked into a black, knee-length pencil skirt, the top has a bow at the collar, cream colored ribbons tail down her bare back.

Simple, black strappy heels. Toes painted a shiny dark red I couldn't help noticing when I picked her up, it's almost as if she put real effort into getting ready. The kind of effort a woman puts into a real date; a real date she's nervous and excited about.

That she anticipated.

I don't know what I was expecting to find when she eagerly swung the door open to her condo earlier, but it's safe to assume: this wasn't it.

She looks incredible. Sweet. Undeniably sexy.

Unattainable yet approachable.

My eyes drop to her tan legs. I want to call them glowing—but that's not right, is it? Glowing? Shit, I don't fucking know. They look freshly shaved and must feel *smooth* if the way she's running her palms around her knees is any indication; up and down her knees in slow circular motions, probably to torture me for coming up with this dumbass idea in the first place.

I give those legs another sidelong glance, trying to erase the desire I feel for her from altering my expression. It remains pleasant. Passive.

Another quick glance as Daphne idly traces her knee cap with the tip of a forefinger has me hoarsely clearing my throat because, *dammit, stop touching your legs.*

Tightening my grip on the steering column, I focus on the road and pull onto the highway, blowing out a pent up puff of air.

I should have just told my mom I wasn't bringing a date. Or been more firm in my resolve that Daphne is just a friend. But can someone be your friend when you've only met twice? I might not be a rocket scientist in the female department, but somehow, even I doubt it.

And yet here we are, on the way to an engagement party.

Where I'll no doubt make an ass of myself.

Her voice jolts me out of my contemplations. "Do you want to go over any details before we get there? Just in case anyone decides to grill us about how we met."

I stare out the windshield, nodding. "Sure. Great idea."

"Alright. I'll start." She pauses with a secret smile. "Let's say we met at a wine bar through mutual friends? That part at least is true… and our first date was the movies."

"StarGate?"

"Yes! Exactly. StarGate." Daphne is quiet for a few seconds, and I can tell that she's thinking. Can see it on her face when I chance a glance her way in the dark cab of my car. Biting down on her lower lip, she hums to herself before asking, "Where should our second date be?" Her head gives a shake, her long, loose brown hair swaying. "Wait. I meant, where should we *say* it was?"

I might be wicked smart, but I'm a guy, so I say, "Uh…"

Daphne laughs and her hand hits my thigh with a teasing tap. It lingers there before returning to her lap. "*Uh*? You're hopeless, do you know that?"

I stare down at my pants, at the thigh that's now singing beneath my dark gray slacks from her touch.

"Do you really think anyone is going to ask where we had our second date? I mean, a continuous line of questioning is kind of rude, don't you think?"

I snort. "That's not going to stop my cousin Elliot from asking shit tons of inappropriate questions. He has no boundaries."

Daphne tilts her head and studies me back in the dark. The lights from the center median on the highway illuminate the cab, her glossy lips shining—and like beacons in the night, my eyes are drawn to them. She licks them.

"Elliot sounds charming."

"He's not a bad guy—not really. He just has no filter."

"What about your other family. I'm kind of nervous to meet your mom and sisters. I'm going to feel horrible lying to them."

"Sorry about dragging you into this. I just think my mom wasn't in the frame of mind to believe me, and instead of arguing with her about having a girlfriend, it's seriously just easier to bring you. My mom hears what she wants to hear. As awkward as it's going to be for you, this is the story of my life."

"Awkward for me?"

"Yeah." I glance at her. "Faking it. Pretending to like me. Pretending to be attracted to me." With a self-deprecating chuckle, my finger pushes my black glasses up the bridge of my nose. "Let's see how good an actress you are."

I find the exit ramp.

Take a right at the light.

Pretend not to be affected by the downturn of her lips.

Daphne

Stupid boy.

I should tell him I don't *have* to pretend.

That I *am* attracted to him.

That I do like him.

That if he'd only asked me on a real date, I would have said yes.

Yes, Dexter, I'd love to go to dinner with you!

Yes, Dexter, I'd love to see another movie.

Yes, Dexter, I'd love to…

But instead, he asked me to be his fake girlfriend for one night. Nothing really but an escort—and an unpaid one at that.

I scoff miserably, wondering if he's thought of it that way at all.

Probably not.

I sigh, glancing over at him, the reflection from the street lights whizzing past us reflecting off his glasses, taking note of the way he's concentrating on the road. How he keeps checking his blind spots. How he turns his blinker on every time he changes lanes. How he steals glances at me when he thinks I'm not paying attention.

But that's where he's wrong.

I *am* paying attention.

Have been since I swung open the door of my apartment earlier, eyes damn near bugging out of my head at the sight of him standing there. Preppy. Professional. Nervous.

Wanting to rip his clothes off, beginning with his buttoned up blue dress shirt, I'd start by running my hands up under the rolled up cuffs of his shirt—over his pale but toned forearms.

Tucked into a pair of black pressed slacks, nothing has ever made me hotter than the site of a guy in…

Suspenders.

Yeah. *Suspenders* for God's sake.

I want to snap them.

Run my hands up his chest, under the length of them.

Slowly unbutton his shirt and push the suspenders down his arms—just to see the look on his face.

I train my lecherous eyes back out the window. "What did you tell your mom about me?"

His deep voice fills the cab of his spotlessly clean car. *"Nothing much, to be honest. She was too busy chastising me for keeping you my dirty little secret—she didn't ask for specific details. All she knows is what my Aunt told her."*

A dirty little secret sounds… delightful.

I sigh, wishing I had one.

In the quiet cab of his fancy car, I hear Dexter shrug. Turning so my head faces him, I brush a lock of hair out of my face. Beneath the lamplights on the street, his eyes follow the motion when my hand caresses the side of my face, swiping at my long curls. "Which is what? What did your aunt tell her?"

"Just the facts—that you were polite." Dexter hesitates. "That you're beautiful."

Beautiful; the word lodges itself in my brain and takes root there at the same time my stomach does a summersault; an unexpected, pleased, little flip-flop.

Beautiful. No one has ever called me that before.

Cute? Yes.

Wholesome? Yes.

Girl-next-door adorable? *Unfortunately.*

Does *Dexter* think I'm beautiful, too? I'm not asking to sound conceited, but it crossed my mind after he didn't ask me out that perhaps… he's not attracted to me. Maybe I'm not his type. Maybe he does truly just want to be friends. Play the doting boyfriend for one night—and one night only.

"And head's up—they all think you're Southern, so good luck with that."

"Trust me, I can manage to throw a few *y'alls* into the conversations. Give Aunt Bethany a cheap thrill."

"Oh, I'm sure you can." His grin is lopsided and amused.

"Sugar, y'all are in for a treat."

Dexter clears his throat. "So she knows that, but not much else. And of course, she thinks we've been dating awhile. Which… I apologize for."

I find myself saying, "It's okay," as we pull into the parking lot of a country club. Find myself nervously fussing with the hem of my skirt as he purposefully strides around to my side of the car after we park. Find myself go a little weak in the knees when his hand presses politely into the small of my back, guiding me towards the crowd of people inside.

And when I remove my jacket and he passes it to the coat check, that hand wraps itself around my waist.

I stiffen; but not from displeasure.

From the opposite.

Dexter notices.

"Is this okay? I think it would be weird if I didn't touch you, don't you?"

I do my best to nod, swallowing the lump in my throat. "It's fine. You're right, it would be weird. I mean, if I was your... *girl*friend you would touch me. Act familiar."

He blows out a puff of air—like he's psyching himself up. "Yes. Alright. Good." He babbles. "Just so we're on the same page."

"Dexter, it's fine. I don't mind you touching me." It's going to drive my hormones absolutely ca-ray-zy but, "Truly. I don't mind."

Hell no I don't mind. Not at all—quite the opposite actually.

My eyes roam back to the suspenders.

Ugh.

Excited with this new development, Dexter's stiff arm relaxes, his hand resting on my hip. "You can call me Dex if you want. That's what my friends and family call me."

Nope. Not gonna do it; not when the name Dexter rolls off the tip of my tongue like the last drop of wine from a glass, and gets me hot and bothered in all the wrong places.

I shoot him a cheeky grin. "Maybe. We'll see."

"Is our brother romantic?" One of Dexter's twin sisters asks, leaning on her elbows towards me as dinner plates are set in front of us by the servers. We arrived casually late and were immediately seated at a table for ten, except the rest of his family hasn't joined us yet; it's just myself, Dexter, and his enthusiastic little sisters.

"Tell us the truth." The twins request at the same time, in the same playful voice.

The twins—Lucy and Amelia—are mirror image identical and almost indistinguishable; dark blonde hair, cut into jaunty, matching bobs. Identical almond-shaped eyes. Freckles across the bridge of their noses. Identical smirks with identical dimples.

You get the picture.

Tonight they're wearing the same dress, in different colors, and watching me across the table with such intensity I squirm in my seat. It's disconcerting and a tad bit creepy.

Especially since there's two of them.

"Is he romantic?" I exaggerate a blissful sigh. "Yes. So romantic, aren't you babe?" I pat his hand.

Dexter visibly swallows. "Totally."

"Mom is right." Lucy says. Then, at the same time, they both enthuse, "You're much prettier than Charlotte was."

Charlotte? Was?

"*Was*? Does that mean she's…" Dead? I can't bring myself to finish the sentence.

I'm guessing it's Lucy who laughs. "His ex-girlfriend, silly. She was—"

"—Awful." Amelia finishes.

"Boring." Both twins roll their brown eyes.

"Do you like Star Wars?" Amelia asks at the same time Lucy says, "Dex likes Star Wars."

"Charlotte hated it," they parrot.

Dexter meets my inquisitive gaze, before silencing them. "Guys, stop with all the questions. You're being rude."

To their credit, both twins blush. "Sorry Daphne. We meant it as a—"

"—Compliment." Lucy pokes at the chicken on her dinner plate before shoving it aside and crossing her arms on the tabletop. "So how is our brother romantic? Tell us. He works so much he hardly comes around."

Amelia sets her napkin on the table and scoots her chair closer to mine. "Tell us."

Crap. They're like a tiny twin mafia; they're not playing around. I'm going to have to make something up. "He, well. Dexter is…"

Amelia interrupts with a gasp. "Oh my god, did you hear that? She calls him—"

"—Dexter."

"So cute." They're like an echo.

It's freaky.

A smile tips my lips, and I'm honest. "Your brother is so sweet, and… such a gentleman. One of the nicest guys I've ever met."

Beside me, Dexter lets out a painful groan. "Sweet? *Nice*? That's horrible."

I nudge him with my knee. "Oh stop. It's a compliment."

He's not convinced. "Sweet and nice—exactly what every warm-blooded American guy wants to be called. Haven't you ever heard the phrase 'nice guys finish last?'

Story of my freaking life."

His sisters are watching us now, wide eyed. The one in pink take a long sip from her water glass, while the other one pokes at the chicken on her plate. For once, they're silent.

"Nice guys finish last? That's not true," I argue. "If they finish last, then what am I doing here?"

Dexter's lips purse. I can tell exactly what he's thinking: *you're here because you're doing me a favor.*

I give my head a tiny shake. *That's not true—not true at all.*

He raises an eyebrow skeptically.

I raise mine.

"Someone outgoing and beautiful doesn't do dull and predictable." His voice is low.

"How are you dull?"

Across the table, the twins lean forward in their chairs, hanging on our every word. Every syllable.

Dexter crosses his arms. "I work a lot."

Pfft. "Big deal, so do I."

It's then that Dexter removes his glasses… Transfixed, I watch as he wipes under his eyes before he meets my wide-eyed stare, his gaze boring into me. Long inky black lashes that should be outlawed on a man. Deep brown irises surrounded by tiny flecks of amber.

With his glasses he's adorable.

Without them, Dexter is… is…

Holy. Hot.

I gaze.

I stare.

I gape at him stupidly.

One of the twins coughs to cover a snicker.

The other titters.

My date uses a linen napkin to wipe the lenses, oblivious to my enamored gawking, gives his head a shake, the moment fleeting when he places the glasses back on the bridge of his nose.

"So Daphne, where did my brother take you on your first date?"

I take a sip of wine then to occupy my hands, and buy myself a few extra seconds before responding. "We went to see StarGate," I say truthfully. "Sat in the theater after it was over talking until they kicked us out, didn't we?"

Dexter nods, glasses firmly back in place.

Amelia scrunches up her nose. His sisters are not impressed. "You took her to see *Star*Gate? Lame!"

With a laugh, I add, "Yes, but I happen to be a huge Sci-Fi junkie. So I wasn't horrified—not like you are right now."

The twins peer at us warily, giving each other sidelong glances. "What about your second date."

"Our second date?"

Shoot, Dexter and I discussed this in the car on the way here, didn't we? Crap, where did we say we went on our second date? With his sisters aiming their focus on me with laser beam accuracy, suddenly I can't remember. Or we hadn't thought this far ahead.

"We... our second date?"

Lucy's eyes are definitely narrowed doubtfully. "You *can't* remember where your second date was?"

Dexter pushes out a laugh. "Was it so boring that you've already forgotten?" His hand brushes my palm affectionately—the way a real boyfriend would do. "We went to a wine bar."

The twins scrunch up their noses. "You said you *met* at a wine bar. So did you meet there, or take her there on your second date?"

They wait.

"You know what? I'm twenty-six years old—you don't get to cross-examine me, questioning my motives. You're fifteen."

"Sixteen in less than three weeks," they clarify.

"That's not my point—"

"Aww Dex, you should see yourself, all flustered." Amelia cuts him off, preening happily before whipping out her cell and snapping a duck face selfie. "You're—"

"—So adorable."

"Dex, are you going to dance with her after dinner?" Amelia asks at the same time Lucy says, "They're setting up now and starting after dinner."

They both sigh. "Before dessert is served."

They sigh again. "Cake."

I can hardly keep up with their conversation.

Lucy pulls out *her* phone, checks the time, and then gestures us closer together. "Okay you little lovebirds. Scootch so I can get a picture."

"Can we post this on our Instagram?" Amelia asks.

"Hashtag *our brother's hot new girlfriend*." Lucy adds while Amelia chastises, "Nobody uses hashtags anymore, Lucy. Nobody."

Lucy ignores her. "But can we?"

"Scoot closer," the voices probe.

We do. We scoot closer, Dexter extending his arm and resting it on my chair back. I lean back, into the crux of his elbow, the heat from his body brushing the skin of my exposed back.

I shiver.

My hand finds his upper thigh—like it would if I was his real girlfriend—and without hesitating, I rest it there and fight the impulse to give it a good squeeze. It would be tacky to feel him up at the dinner table, wouldn't it?

Especially since this isn't a real date.

Right?

I sigh, disappointed, as the flash from the cell goes off.

"Aren't you going to touch her?" His sisters ask him skeptically, clearly disgusted by our lack of PDA.

A look passes between the two of them; a knowing, secretive glance that's slightly disturbing and has me narrowing my green eyes.

"I *am* touching her," Dexter deadpans, flopping his hand near my shoulder. *Near* but not on. "See?"

"Dex," they coax. "This picture is gonna suck if you don't get your faces closer together."

"Oh, God forbid." Sarcasm becomes him.

"Maybe kiss her cheek," one twin suggests playfully with a simper, holding her phone out. They snap a few more selfies before aiming the cell back towards us. "Ready?"

"Closer."

Dexter's chest presses into my back and his hand comes down off the back of my seat. It covers my bare shoulder, solid and big and warm. His thumb caresses back and forth against my skin before he catches himself doing it and stops. Once.

Twice.

I shiver, catching Lucy's knowing grin.

She winks at me above her iPhone.

Why, that sneaky little…
"Smile!"
"Say cheese!"

I beam until my face hurts. Turn my face. Inhale the woodsy, fresh scent of Dexter's freshly shaven neck with no shame. I mean—since it's *right* freaking there. His jaw is so strong and defined it's just *begging* to be sniffed. Begging.

And it smells so…

So.

Good.

Down girl. He's not into you like that.

From the corner of my eye, I catch Lucy nudge Amelia with her elbow, and the pair of them do another series of head nods and eyebrow raises that I've decided must be some weird Twin Speak.

Those two are trouble.

Double trouble.

Six

Dexter

So far, so good.

My parents haven't completely embarrassed me; but then again, not wanting to scare Daphne away, they've given us a wide berth, twins notwithstanding.

Been on their best behavior.

No questions being fired off at a missile-launching pace. No intrusively personal questions. No uncomfortable or inappropriate statements containing the words *marriage, babies, or give me grandbabies*.

Well, unless you count my Aunt Tory telling Daphne the reception hall where her daughter Grace is having her wedding has an opening nineteen months from now—if we hurry, we can still book it.

Only three of every ten statements have been intrusive; I consider those *very* good statistics.

I've managed to shuffle my faux date to the dance floor, away from the inquisition but not the prying eyes; if anything, I've made us more vulnerable to speculation by hauling Daphne to the middle of the ballroom.

Under the dim lights of the crystal chandelier, joy radiates off her. Or maybe it's just the reflection from the hundreds of prisms; either way, Daphne lets me hold her close and twirl her around, giggling at my tragic attempts at humor and grinning up at me at the appropriate times.

The urge to touch her intimately and pull her flush against my body is unbearable.

Either she's truly enjoying herself, or she's a terrific actress.

My cousin Gracie has hired some fancy cover-band from the city, and they're belting out some low-rent version of Photograph by Ed Sheeran. Daphne and I sway in synch along to the beat—her hands lock around my neck in a definitively girlfriendy way.

Contemplating me affectionately, she's acting like she *adores* me. A pink flush on her cheeks and fresh coat of gloss swiped across her lips. The look makes me—

Stop it Dex, this isn't real.

The look *isn't* real.

Because if it was, I would most definitely be dipping my neck and covering her mouth with mine to discover what flavor those glossy lips are.

But I won't.

I won't because that's not what this is—because I didn't have the balls to ask her on a real date.

And that's the pisser of it all.

I scan the room, groaning inwardly at the sight of my Cousin Elliot casually resting his elbows against the wooden counter of the bar. He tips his highball glass and chin as a greeting, his assessment of my date evident all the way across the room. Elliot begins at her feet, his brows raising the longer he studies her perfect figure—her waist, her firm backside. I know the exact moment his perusal reaches her perfect breasts because his lascivious grin widens, dammit.

Our eyes meet.

My cousin gives me another cocky nod as my hands skim Daphne's bare back, his mouth tipping into a toothy grin as he pushes himself away from the bar top. Turning towards the bartender, he throws down a few singles, says a few parting words, smacks our Uncle Dave on the back, and grabs his glass, weaving his way through the crowded reception room.

Towards us.

Determined.

Shit.

I knew he wouldn't be able to resist.

Now, if Daphne was plain and unattractive this would be a different story.

But she's not.

She's gorgeous and sexy and out of my league. What's worse, Elliot fucking knows it; he plans to take full advantage.

"My cousin is on his way over." I grumble, impulsively raising my hand to smooth it down Daphne's long, wavy hair. It feels like I imagine spun silk to feel— like warm water cascading in a languid, steady stream through my fingers—and smells a whole hellova lot better. Like shampoo and honey and baby powder.

So good.

So *not* mine.

Daphne

Elliot is a total douche.

I know it's not fair to run comparisons—particularly on someone I haven't met—but it's obvious Dexter and his cousin fell off different branches of the family tree: they are the complete opposites. Where Dexter is kind, caring and approachably handsome, Elliot is *in your face* good-looking. Cocky. Spray tanned. Manwhore with a heart of gold. A schmoozer used to gaining anything he wants from women.

Used to getting *in* anyone and *every*one's panties.

Gross, did I just say panties?

Ew.

I've met a hundred Elliot Ryan's in my short lifetime and I've no doubt I'll meet more; he is certainly no novelty.

Not to me, anyways.

He's sizing me up as a potential prospect even as he walks towards us, a knowing glint in his arrogant eye—he thinks I'm going to be charmed by his bullshit. His body.

His face.

He's so conceited and full of himself he thinks I'll ditch Dexter and leave here with him. Unfortunately for Elliot, I am immune and speak *fluent* douche.

Our dance near an end, Dexter relaxes his grip as his

cousin approaches with a swagger, and I mournfully unclasp my hands from their spot around his neck. Standing steadfastly beside him, I reach between our bodies to grapple for his hand, lacing our fingers together in a show of solidarity.

Plus, I *really* want to touch him.

He looks down at our joined hands surprised when I give them a flirty little squeeze.

"Hey cuz, pardon the interruption." Elliot is so full of shit I want to burst out laughing. He's not one bit sorry—he's rude. "Aunt Bethany said you brought a new girlfriend tonight, but I had to see it myself."

His mouth is speaking to Dexter, but his interest clearly lies with me. "And you must be…?"

"Elliot, this is Daphne. Daff, this is my cousin, Elliot."

Daff? Oh brother, he's pulling out the pet names?

"Hi, pleased to meet you. I'd shake your hand, but as you can see, it's otherwise occupied." I slouch on my heel, leaning on Dexter for support. He immediately releases my hand to slide his arm around my waist, pulling me flush into his body. Shamelessly, I return the favor, hugging my date's trim waist, letting my other palm rest on the flat of his abs.

I feel them flex under my fingers, and give them a playful little tickle.

"Dexter and Daphne. The Double D's, get it?" Elliot jokes, pasting a megawatt grin across his handsome face. So good-looking. So pleasant. *So fake*. "Hey man—sorry about standing you up at the wine bar the other weekend after the golf tournament. I didn't mean to leave you hanging."

His eyes never leave my face.

"No worries. It all worked out." Dexter's hand gives me a squeeze. "Besides, I wasn't there entirely alone."

Elliot cocks his head thoughtfully to study us. I can almost hear the cogs in his brain working overtime. Almost. "Yeah, I heard that's where the two of you met."

"Yup, I'm a lucky guy." Dexter kisses the top of my head.

Elliot squints at us. "Seriously though. The two of you are dating?"

Seriously though? Could he be any less subtle?

Dickhead.

"Well, the sparks *really* flew when we bumped into each other a few days later." I look up into Dexter's kind eyes. "Remember? You came to my rescue at the movie theater?"

"Was he wearing a bow tie?" Elliot laughs—a booming, obnoxious, and patronizing snort, revealing the dark side of his personality.

Asshole.

There was only one way to wipe that smirk off his face.

"Wearing a bow tie?" I ask purposefully. Slowly. "Well... he *was* wearing one at the *beginning* of the night. But I had it on in the morning." I push out a giggle. "Sometimes all I have on are his glasses, isn't that right babe?"

Bashfully in Elliot's direction, I demure. "I love his glasses, don't you?"

Unable to control myself, I rise onto my tip-toes and kiss the underside of Dexter's chin. My lips linger, the tip of my nose giving his jaw a little nudge.

Mmm. He smells heavenly. Divine.

"Wait." Elliot looks confused. "Hey man, am I seriously interrupting something? You're not fucking around?"

A laugh escapes my lips. "We were dancing! Of course you're interrupting something."

Idiot.

"Yeah *man*, we'll catch you later at the bar for a round, Ellie. Your treat." Dexter nuzzles my hair before spinning me around. "Right now I'm going to finish out this set with my gorgeous date."

"Sorry Elliot." Breathlessly, I don't take my eyes off Dexter's face. "You're gonna have to excuse us—I just want to be alone with these sexy suspenders. I've been *dying* to run my hands under them all night."

I shoot my date a pointed look. "*All* night."

To emphasize my point, the arms wrapped around his waist snake up the front of his button-down shirt, the pads of my palms slowly move up and under his blue paisley suspenders.

"I-I.." he stutters, pushing up his glasses with the tip of his forefinger. "You *like* these?"

He's genuinely shocked.

"No, I *love* them." I confess, biting down on my lower lip. "Why did you wear them if not to drive me insane?"

His mouth opens but no sound comes out. We're the only two people on the dance floor *not* dancing; the only two people on the dance floor, surrounded by his family and cousin Grace's good friends.

The only two people that matter; right here.

Right now.

Or maybe it's just me.

My fake date is kind of hard to read; he's spent more time being chivalrous and gentlemanly than flirty. He hasn't made one single overture. Not one single advance. Hasn't touched me in a way that was anything but friendly.

Unfortunately.

And yet…

It's his eyes that give him away. They're interested. Intrigued.

Something in his eyes…

He *longs* for me.

I can see it.

But.

There's something else I see reflected in his dark, brown eyes; doubt. For himself and my attraction to him.

So that *longing*?

He won't do anything about it.

"You know how ridiculous the whole thing is, right?" I'm in my apartment, make-up removed, sitting cross-legged in the center of my big, fluffy bed. I couldn't resist a phone call to Tabitha with a recap of the past several days; the movie. The meeting at the coffee shop where Dexter propositioned me.

The engagement party.

"I don't understand why he didn't just ask you to be his date. It makes *no* sense." I can hear Tabitha shuffling around her kitchen, a pan going into the sink followed by running water.

I throw myself back, sinking into my pillows and staring up at the ceiling. "Right? The whole fake date thing was dumb. All it managed to do was fire up my imagination. It's running wild. You know how I always want what I can't have? Ugh, his lack of interest is driving me crazy."

"I wouldn't call it lack of interest; I'd call it a lack of cojones."

I ignore her flippant remark and prattle on. "Besides, what is this—a Made for TV movie? What are we, in high school?"

On the other end of the line, she's speaking around her toothbrush. "Yeah, it was pretty immature." She takes it out of her mouth to say, "But maybe…"

My best friend's voice trails off.

"Maybe *what*? I'm hanging on your every word here."

"Well, maybe—just maybe—he's intimidated by you and doesn't want to be rejected. That's Collin's theory, and I happen to agree with him. You can be pretty intimidating, Daphne."

I consider this.

I'm not shy or reserved, and if I'm being brutally honest, I haven't broken any mirrors lately.

"Okay, yes. That's a possibility." I pause before adding more information. "But I'm *pretty* sure he was going to ask me out after the movie. I'd bet my favorite yoga pants on it."

"He was spooked by his aunt," Tabitha declares with authority. I can picture her nodding in agreement. "And now he's too chicken shit—" She stops mid-sentence. "Tell the truth; do you *really* want to date a guy like that, though? Not enough balls to ask you on a real date? It's kind of *wimpy*."

I've debated this a million times in my head so I immediately jump to his defense. "Jeez Tabitha, just because he's not humping my leg or sending me dick pics doesn't make him a wimp."

She huffs indignantly. "Please don't call him *sensitive*. That's way worse."

I chuckle. "No, he's not *that* nice. I mean—he is, but he also has a smart mouth on him, too; it's sexy."

His smart mouth.

Those lips.

"Sexy Dexy," Tabitha croons into the receiver. "You know, I bet he's got a lot of pent-up sexual repression."

My ears perk up. "Ya think?"

"Oh *yeah*, definitely." Tabitha breaths seductively. "You said yourself he's a thinker—he's probably *thinking* of all the ways to *do* you."

God I hope so.

"No doubt he's got himself convinced you're out of his league."

I scoff at this. "He couldn't be more wrong."

"Then prove it. Show him he's wrong."

"I can't," I whine like a baby. "He put me in the Friend-Zone."

Tabitha sighs impatiently. "No, he put *him*self there. Now *you* need to take him out."

"Hmmm, we'll see…"

"I'm sorry, what was that? You need. To take. Him. Out."

"Have you always been this bossy?"

"No, it's something new I'm trying out." I can practically hear her rolling her blue eyes.

"Wow, sarcastic, too. Collin's one lucky guy."

Tabitha releases a breathy laugh. "Sweetie. If you like him, just do it; make a move. Don't wait until your ovaries dry up."

Seven

Daphne

It turns out, I don't have to make the first move. Instead, the opportunity to see Dexter falls into my lap in the form of two brown haired, mischievous teenage twins.

Who apparently *really,* really like me.

A lot.

Enough to *steal* my number out of Dexter's phone during the engagement party and message me on the sly behind his back, bless their heartless, black little souls. Was it inappropriate for them to text me without telling their brother? Without a doubt—*so* inappropriate.

Was it inappropriate for them to invite me to their Mom's house for their annual birthday cookie bake? *So* inappropriate.

Do I care?

Um, no.

Why? Because I want to see him again—and if Dexter Ryan isn't going to make a move on me, I'm not above resorting to my own brand of passive aggressive man-hunting.

Besides, *I was invited.*

Sure, I'll probably regret the decision to randomly show up at his mom's house, but as I reach behind my waist to tie the dainty, yellow polka dot apron strings in a bow, all I can think is the possibility that Dexter will walk through that front door.

I know the twins said they hadn't told him I was coming, but… a girl can dream. Plus, I'm no expert on twins, but these girls are pretty shady; I'm pretty sure they plan sketchy plots like this on a regular basis.

Mrs. Ryan—Georgia—has all the ingredients set on the counter by the time I arrive; everything pre-measured, eggs counted out, bowls at the ready. She's even separated the buttercream frosting into three metal mixing bowls, in the twins' three favorite colors: pink, lavender, and lime green.

Fluttering around the kitchen, Georgia hands me a pot-holder, directing me to check on the twelve sugar cookies shaped like the number sixteen, already in the oven.

They're a light golden brown and ready to come out.

They smell divine.

"You know, we've been baking birthday cookies for the twins for five years," she explains, sliding one cookie sheet out of the oven and another one in. "We stopped doing cake after their eleventh birthday—the year they got into a huge fight over which flavor; marble or red velvet."

Amelia laughs. "What a dumb thing to fight about." I know it's her because there's a monogram with her initials on the pocket of her baby blue tee shirt.

I make a mental note: Amelia—blue monogrammed tee shirt and jeans. Lucy: pajama bottoms and tank top.

Got it.

"Tossing sprinkles everywhere," Lucy adds.

"My husband was furious. Cake all over the kitchen," Georgia laughs at the memory with a smile, handing me a spatula. "Anyway, we decided that year to make cookies the birthday tradition. Easier and cleaner. Their friends love them during lunch, and I don't have to listen to the bickering."

"It's not bickering," Amelia disagrees. "It's—"

"—Debating."

"Well it's obnoxious," their mom says as we start to remove the cookies from the cookie sheets. Mrs. Ryan has a cooling rack on the counter. "Sweetie, would you hand me the wax paper?"

I mentally choose a cookie from the rack, anticipation making my stomach growl.

"She's talking to you," Lucy says, nudging me in the ribs with her pointy adolescent elbow. "Wax paper."

"Oh, sorry!" I apologize, springing into action.

"Shake a tail feather," Amelia teases. "No slacking on this job. We're known for our freakishly delicious birthday cookies."

"Freakishly large." Lucy smiles, going in to dip her finger in the pale pink frosting. Amelia slaps her hand away, pure disgust etched on her face.

"Stop. That's gross."

"Chill out, I washed my hands," Lucy rolls her eyes. "Hey, did you know Dex always complains because Mom never baked *him* special cookies—"

"—What did he want with cookies, anyway? He's a guy."

"Girls!" Georgia laughs. "I made him *cake*! Besides, when he was younger, we didn't have the money. All these ingredients you're throwing on each other for fun aren't cheap."

She's right; flour and sugar are everywhere, including on me. In my hair, on my clothes. I run a hand down the dainty, vintage apron wrapped around my waist, flattening out the wrinkles.

I love this stupid thing; I wonder if I could get away with wearing an apron on a regular basis as I lean against the counter, fingering several thin, charms on my necklace—one is a tiny, gold wishbone my sister bought me when I graduated from college two years ago, and I'm seldom without it.

When we were younger, my dad was big into duck hunting.

He would come home with the birds (gross, I know) and my mom would dress them for dinner, saving the wishbone for my sister, Morgan, and I to pull apart after our evening meal.

A friendly little competition, if I was lucky enough to snap off the wishbone, I usually said a prayer for stupid, trivial things; new clothes. A cool car. But the older I grew, my wishes became more altruistic; a steady job. Healthy family. Loyal friends.

I adore wishbones, just like I love throwing pennies into a wishing well, and making wishes when the clock strikes eleven-eleven.

Childish? Maybe.

But something so small has always filled me with tremendous hope; and I always hoped for love. No, not hoped—*wished*. Wished it from the depths of my soul.

Yeah, I get it; we're living in a world where feminism and female independence is a valuable asset. Two values that women have fought for centuries to obtain—but that doesn't make me want someone to share my life with any less.

Coming home to an empty apartment with no cat, no dog, or companionship *sucks.*

The twins' squabbling interrupts my daydreaming.

"We *know* the ingredients aren't cheap, Mom." The twins emphasize the same word, and reach for the jar of tiny purple candies at the same time, too.

"Then stop wasting sprinkles," Georgia chastises.

The twins exchange bemused glances. "But it's fun."

Inside the back pocket of my jeans, my phone vibrates, its chirpy little buzzing. I excuse myself to use the bathroom.

Tabitha: *Hey, what are you doing today?*

Me: *Playing baker—making delicious, gourmet cookies.*

Tabitha: *Shut up. LOL. For real though, what are you doing today?*

Me: *Why are you laughing?! That's what I'm doing!*

Tabitha: *This I gotta see; Collin's taking Greyson to pick out their parents' anniversary gift, then they're going* *to dinner. I'm bored. Let me jump in the shower quick and I'll be over in 20 minutes.*

Tabitha: *I wanna eat COOKIES!!!!*

Me: *NO! Don't! I'm not home…*

Tabitha: *Ugh, well that sucks! So where ARE you?*

Me: *I'm… at Dexter's, um… Mom's house?*

Tabitha: *WHAT??? Stop it, you are not.*

Me: *Shit, I shouldn't have told you.*

Tabitha: *Well that escalated quickly! I thought you weren't dating! Seriously though, what the HELL ARE YOU DOING AT HIS MOM'S HOUSE BAKING COOKIES?*

Me: *His sisters texted me and wanted me to bake with them today—they really like me, I guess, and they're young. What was I supposed to say???*

Tabitha: *Wait, is this the twins?*

Me: *Yeah.*

Tabitha: *How bout "Sorry twinsies! I might be lusting after your nerdy brother, but I'm NOT ACTUALLY DATING HIM!" There. That's what you could say.*

Me: **rolling my eyes* Oh, like it's that easy.*

Tabitha: *Yeah, it is actually. You just type it out and hit SEND. Please tell me Dexter is there with you.*

Me: *Um. No. He went in to work today, but I think one of the twins texted him. They were being really weird and sneaky, giggling over their phone a few minutes ago.*

Tabitha: *Sexer Dexer!*

Me: *That nickname is worse than Sexy Dexy.*

Tabitha: *I still can't believe you're at his mom's house. I'm literally dead over here. Dying. You have some lady balls. And also…super creepy.*

Me: *You told me to take him out of the friend zone!*

Tabitha: *Well yeah! But not like THIS!*

Tabitha: *Jeez Daff, the guy is going to piss his khakis when he finds you in his mom's kitchen baking it up with his family. That guy does NOT strike me as the type that likes surprises...*

Dexter

I don't like surprises.

Daphne Winthrop is the last person on Earth I expect to see when I walk into my Mom's house. Her kitchen. And yet—there she is. Standing among the chaos, wielding a spatula and wearing the cutest fucking shamefaced expression I've ever seen.

And the sexiest fucking apron.

Stunned from shock and faltering beneath the threshold, I take in the rest of her from head to toe; long hair in a pretty little ponytail. Silver hoop earrings. Gray short sleeve tee shirt over faded skinny jeans with ripped up knees, a yellow and white polka dot apron is tied around her slim waist.

Bare feet with bubble-gum pink nails.

Those cute feet.

I stare at those pink nails dumbly until she wiggles her toes, and slowly raise my head to meet her gaze.

"Hi." Her mouth tips into a bashful little smile.

What is she doing in my Mom's kitchen? I mean—obviously she's baking, but… what the hell is she doing in my mom's kitchen?

My mom rolls her eyes. "Dex you're being weird. Don't just stand there gawking at the poor girl. Come in here and give her a proper hello."

Still, I'm rooted to the spot. "What's... going on?"

What is she doing in my Mom's kitchen?

Mom ignores me. "Don't be rude. And can you grab us the broom from the hall closet since you're just standing there? Make yourself useful."

"It's okay Georgia," Daphne lays the utensil on the counter next to a black wire cookie rack I've seen on my mom's counter a thousand times, wipes her hands on the apron around her waist, and starts towards me. "He's just surprised to see me, that's all. I didn't tell him I was coming over."

It doesn't escape my notice that she's calling my mom Georgia with familiarity. My brows shoot into my hairline as Daphne reaches me, eyes sparkling with mischief. She goes up on the balls of her feet and leans in.

"Surprise?"

Her words are a light whisper right in the sensitive spot beneath my ear, the tip of her nose brushing gently against my lobe. Her warm breath rests a heartbeat too long on my skin to be accidental, and when she pulls away, I raise my hand.

"You have a little flour... right... there." I brush it off her cheek with a slow, gentle swipe.

She bites her lower lip demurely. "I haven't greeted you properly, have I?" Her soft lips connect to my jaw line the briefest of seconds; so quickly I might have imagined it.

"Hi."

Confused *as shit* but smiling like an idiot, I finally return her greeting. "Hi."

Daphne reaches up, removes my old University baseball hat, and runs her fingers over my scalp, giving my hair a tussle.

Christ her fingers feel good; *too* fucking good.

"The twins texted me an invite to help bake their birthday cookies; I could hardly say no," she says by way of explanation. "I didn't realize it would be quite this big a production."

I adjust my glasses and narrow my eyes.

My sisters—who aren't usually this quiet—hum happily over near the sink, sneaking covert glances over their shoulders and doing that weird telepathic Twin Speak crap they do when they don't want to talk out loud. Or are up to no good.

I stare the twins down hard.

"*Gee*, what a coincidence. Because they texted me, too. An S.O.S—something about needing help with their *economics* homework."

The girls make a display of loudly running the faucet, filling the sink with suds, clanking dishes around in the water, and avoiding my suspicious gaze.

"Hey, don't ignore me." I cross my arms, moving towards my younger sisters. "Correct me if I'm wrong, but I believe the phrase you used in the text was *DEFCON 5 Level Economics shit only you can help us with*. Do I have that right Lucy? Econ shit?" I use air quotes to illustrate my point, but they're determined to ignore me.

Silence.

"Do you even *take* economics?" I practically shout.

Lucy's shoulders shake with merriment as Amelia splashes her with bubbles. "*Moron*. I knew you'd get us into trouble."

"It was your idea!"

Now they're openly bickering, and once they get

started…

"Shut *up* Amelia. Seriously. This was *your* idea—"

"You don't have to *do* everything I *tell* you to do, *Lucy*, God! Be a think-for-yourselfer every once in a while—"

"—You're so annoying. Stop making that ugly face at me—"

"—This is *your* ugly face. *Duh.*"

My mom has this shrill, nervous laugh she employs when she panics—the situations usually involve my sisters, their weird twin crap, or the occasional fight between my aunts—to break up the tension.

She unleashes it now.

Anxiously walking up behind Daphne, she begins hastily loosening the apron strings behind her back while my sisters continue arguing back-and-forth. Daphne's arms go up as Mom quickly removes the apron, draping it over her arm and shooing at us. "There now! Dexter, sweetie, now's a good time for you to take Daphne somewhere nice. Run along. Daphne, you can leave your car here and come grab it later. Shoo! Go!"

Lucy flicks Amelia with sudsy water.

My mom's voice gets louder. "Run along now. We'll finish this up later. The twins can clean up this mess; the two of you can go grab an early dinner if you get moving."

Before I can object, Daphne is being ushered into her jacket, shoes are being laid at her bare feet, and we're being escorted towards the front door.

Practically pushed out into the cold.

Porch light goes on.

Just as the door is being closed behind us with a resounding thud and the deadbolt slides into place, from the corner of my eye I catch sight of the twins through the crack—high-fiving.

Those little, meddling—

"I think your mom and sisters are playing matchmaker," Daphne says quietly beside me once we're standing on the porch, stuffing her hands in her pockets to keep them warm. The air is so chilly we can see our breath.

"They already think we're dating." I point out.

Daphne gives a little nod, hands sinking deeper into her pockets. "Maybe."

My gaze lands on the SUV I drove tonight instead of my Audi; and for once I'm glad for it. With the weather turning, it's the safer of my two vehicles.

Still, not wanting to be presumptuous, I delay moving towards it.

Daphne does not. "Well, I guess we can't stand out here all night; we'll freeze. We could go... do something?"

Her voice is encouraging. Excited.

Naw. Can't be.

"But it's Saturday."

Tilting her chin up, she regards me under the glow from my parents' porch light. Her bright green eyes are sparkling up at me. "True. It *is* Saturday. But can you think of a better place to be right now? I can't."

It sounds like she's flirting.

"You know, there's a reason I didn't tell your sisters no."

Oh jeez—she's definitely flirting.

Daphne Winthrop is standing on my mother's porch on a Saturday night, flirting. With me. I roll this concept around in my head, mentally calculating what little I know about women and trying to determine her motives.

If I didn't know any better, I would think she wanted …

Shit.

Me.

In the cool night air, I give my head a shake; it makes no sense. None at all.

Not to be rude, but, "Daphne, why are you here?" I ask cautiously. Deliberately.

"I-I was invited."

"Okay." My eyes scan the empty yard and I exhale, the air from my warm breath forming another gray puff of smoke. "That's it? That's the reason?"

I'm not playing dumb; I genuinely can't figure out her motives.

"I'm sorry." She looks down at her feet, studying the wooden floor boards of the deck below us. Her voice is small. "I wasn't thinking; honestly, I didn't have plans other than *maybe* going to another movie by myself and stuffing my face with popcorn, and your family is so wonderful. Plus…"

Her voice trails off.

"Plus… *what*?" I'm desperate for her to finish that sentence; it holds so much possibility.

Daphne looks up and out into the dark side yard. "Plus. I—This is going to sound so lame."

God I want to reach out and touch her. "No it won't."

"I thought we could be friends."

Friends.

Friends?

Fuck.

Hey, I'm a smart guy—not *completely* delusional—

and know my chances of dating someone like Daphne Winthrop are slim to none; but a guy can dream. It's not like I'm lying in bed at night, closing my eyes and jerking-off while picturing her naked in my mind.

Okay, I *am*—but it was only once.

Fine. Three times.

With a resound sigh, I motion towards my car. "Hungry?"

She gives me a megawatt smile, her green eyes shining under the soft glow of the lamp light.

Gorgeous.

"*Starving.*"

"Fine, let's go get something to eat. *Friend.*"

Eight

Daphne

I thought we could be friends.
  Just friends?
  Why would I even say something like that?
I am such a liar.

Nine

Dexter

The twins are spying.

When we come back to my parents' place after our brief dinner, they're barely concealed behind the sheer curtains draped across their second story window; their nosey silhouettes are pressed against the glass conspicuously, glaringly obvious given the fact they never shut the lights off in their shared bedroom.

The sheers flutter, pulled back, whipping back and forth when one twin shoves the other aside, vying for more window space. I can't tell who is who, but when one gets jostled back, more prodding ensues.

They'll *never* make it in espionage.

I don't fight back the chuckle at their blatant lack of stealth; amused, I can't even muster up the energy to be irritated.

Or maybe I'm just happy.

Shit, that's got to be it.

Daphne and I walk unhurriedly through my parents' manicured lawn to the car parked in the shadows next to the house. Her body shivers.

"Cold?"

"Yeah, kind of. *Brrrr*. I have to remember mittens next time I leave the house with the seasons changing."

"I have some in my car—let me go grab them."

"Gosh, no! That's okay," she protests—but I'm already halfway across the lawn to my car, pulling open the door and digging through the glove box to retrieve the gloves.

Ah, here they are.

I hold up them up for inspection, blowing inside one, then the other, to warm them as I jog back to Daphne. Even in the dim shadows I can see her beaming when I hold out the first glove.

I hold it steady as she slides her hands in to each one.

She gives her hands a wiggle, smile widening. "Thank you."

The yard is quiet; we have no neighbors and my parents live on a wooded lot. Besides my snooping fifteen-year-old sisters spying from upstairs, we're completely alone.

"You're welcome."

She leans her shoulder against the door of her silver car, nothing but the sound of our breathing and the jingling of her cars keys in the still night air.

I clear my throat. "So."

"*So…*" Daphne shifts on her heels, dragging out the word like it's actually a question. It sounds diminutively more meaningful than a regular *so*, so... I'm actually really confused.

I'm tempted to repeat the word one more time, but fight the power. Removing my glasses, I lift the hem of my blue cable knit sweater to clean the lenses.

Instinctually, I feel Daphne move in closer; my personal space instantly becomes warmer.

"Can you see without those?"

I chuckle, the sound reverberating against the silence, and tease, "I can see *you*, if that's what you were wondering."

Even without my glasses, I can see her biting down on that pouty lower lip with her teeth to hide a shy smile. She cocks her head up at me. "Maybe it was."

I don't know how to respond to that.

"Aren't you curious, Dexter?" She whispers in the shadow, her warm breath forming a small puff of steam around her words in the cold, night air.

"Curious about what?"

God, even *I* can hear how fucking ridiculous that sounds. *Curious about what?* my inner thoughts mock. My friend Collin would be kicking my ass right now if he heard how much I sounded like a pussy. I have no game when it comes to women.

"Curious about... nothing." Daphne fakes a laugh, giving her head a little shake. "Nothing."

Except it doesn't feel like nothing. It sounds like she's asking for something in a language I don't speak. And I might not know shit about women, but I know that right now, she's flirting with me.

Or not.

Shit, I can't tell.

"Thanks for putting up with me tonight." She goes for the door handle of her car, pausing before pulling it open. "Your family is pretty… spectacular. I know you weren't expecting me today, so it was a relief when you didn't freak out."

"No problem. Don't worry about it."

"Right. Well…" Daphne lowers herself into the driver's seat, buckles her seat belt, and looks up at me with those eyes. Those dejected green eyes. "Good night, Dexter."

I push the glasses up the bridge of my nose. "Night."

Watching as she pulls out of the drive and her taillights slowly fade into the dark distance, I turn, glancing up towards the twins' bedroom window. Arms crossed, their double disappointment is palpable even from two stories up.

Fuck.

Ten

Dexter

"Sir?" Vanessa's voice crackles out of the intercom sitting on my desk. Sir? It still makes me cringe every time she or anyone from the office calls me that moniker. I'm twenty-six for Christ Sake; I might be one of the youngest junior traders for my company, but when Vanessa calls me Sir, I always expect my dad to come waltzing into the room.

"I have Brian Sullivan on hold from Nordic Acuities." Vanessa prods. "He hasn't heard a response on the email he sent through yesterday, and called to verify you'd responded. Can you check your outgoing messages and get back to me?"

I lean forward, tapping on the TALK button. "Yup. I'll do it now."

Tapping on my mouse, I open Outlook and go straight

to the outgoing mail.

Sent to: Collin Keller, Calvin Thompson. Subject: Joke of the day.
Sent to: Brian Sullivan. Subject: Merger

The wheels of my desk chair swivel as I roll back towards the intercom button. "Vanessa? It's still in the queue. Please call Brian and tell him I'm re-sending it right over."

"Thank you, Sir."

"Please stop calling me Sir—I'm only fifteen years younger than you."

"I'll stop calling you Sir when you head back to being an intern on the lower floors. Sir." I can hear her smirking.

Smart ass.

"Fine." I shift in my seat, hand hovering about the mouse pad. "I'm going to take forty-five minutes for lunch today, but I'm eating at my desk. Hold any correspondence until," I glance at my clock. "Until one thirty, please."

The intercom continues to crackle. And chuckle. "Got it."

My fingers move the cursor over my screen, moving to the corner of the monitor to close the window, eyes continuously scanning the screen. They land on the joke I'd sent Collin this morning, the brief memo mentioning a clients no-contact policy.

My message to Daphne.

As I—

Wait.

Rewind.

My eyes do a double take, my head actually swiveling

despite the screen being dead center in front of me.

Message to *Daphne*? What the shit is this?

Clicking the message open, my heart actually begins rapidly palpitating—so strong I can feel it beating in my neck.

Holy Christ.

To: dwinthrop_vp@publicrelations.info
From: DRyan@halyarcapitolinvsec.co
Subject:

Hello Daphne. I hope you had a lovely evening the other night after making cookies with my awesome sisters. They had a blast with you. I'm sorry I suck and let you drive away without asking you on a date. I was wondering if you'd be at their actual birthday party in two weeks. It's on a Sunday. I'm too shy and lame to tell you in person, but I think you're beautiful. I have horrible luck with girls because as you noticed I'm kind of a geek but not as boring as people think I am. For example, I love hiking in the mountains and ski trips. I would never say this to your face.

Yours Truly,
Dexter Ryan

I squint at the screen, reading and re-reading, praying to God that I'm not seeing what I'm actually seeing.

Too shy and lame?

What in the actual shit is this?

WHAT IN THE ACTUAL SHIT IS THIS?

Not only did I *not* send this, it sounds like a fucking fifteen-year old teenager wrote it—specifically *two* of them—and makes me look like a freaking moron. My face burns scarlet and my knuckles, which aren't touching any keys, are white.

White.

This positively *reeks* with the stench of Lucy and Amelia. Those nosey, meddling, conniving little brats have done some really stupid shit in their lives—like the time they switched places so Lucy could take an Algebra exam for Amelia but forgot to swap outfits.

They're constantly trying to Parent Trap unsuspecting people.

And I have no clue what that even means.

Those pranks were bad, but interfering in my personal business is going too far. I'm going to ring their scrawny, pubescent necks when I get my hands on those two.

I cannot even control my breathing, and although I don't have asthma, it feels like I'm having an asthma attack. Or a panic attack.

Daphne *read* this shit. Fucking read it.

How do I know? My *reads* are on. Read: 10:37am

She probably thinks I'm a blabbering idiot.

My stomach drops.

I take a few calming breaths—then a few more—before cracking my knuckles and suspend my hands above the keyboard, at the ready. How do I reply? What the hell do I say that's not going to sound *asinine*? Do I apologize? Explain that my darling sisters hacked my phone when I was home and sent the email for me? Yeah. Cause that's not going to sound idiotic and implausible.

My hands get buried in my hair and I tug.

How did they even manage it?

Those little…

Without further ado, my fingers nimbly fly over the keyboard, tapping out the following, professional and apologetic reply to Daphne.

To: dwinthrop_vp@publicrelations.info
From: DRyan@halyarcapitolinvsec.co
Subject: My sincerest apologies

Hello, Daphne. In regards to the recent message sent to your email account from mine; that note was sent by my sisters, in an obviously immature attempt to get your attention. It was obviously poor manners and an error in judgment on their part. I apologize for any level of embarrassment you might have felt receiving it, which may far exceed mine. Furthermore—

I'm distracted momentarily by the phone next to the computer buzzing, the email notification in the top left corner lighting up with a soft blue blinking light.

Shit. That could be Brian Sullivan already replying.

I lift the cell, swiping the screen down and tap to open the email browser.

For the second time in a short timeframe, my stomach drops as I stare at Daphne Winthrop's email address in my inbox, the Subject line reading: *I don't know what to say.*

I can't make myself tap her reply open it; I cannot.

Instead, I sit back in my desk chair palming the phone in my right hand and staring at that email address and short fucking sentence, trying to decipher what it could mean without opening the message.

I don't know what to say other than:

… that letter you sent had to have been a joke.

... I can't believe a grown-ass man wrote that.

... you should be embarrassed and *never* allowed near woman.

Shit, what does it actually say? I'm dying to open it at the same time I dread it. My thumb hovers, millimeters from an answer. I push the black glasses I wear to work up my nose, a thin layer of perspiration dampening my forehead.

Christ I'm pitiful.

Clicking my phone off, I set it on my desktop and frown scornfully, while the apology message I'd been composing to Daphne looms in front of me on the screen of my laptop. Mocking.

I hit 'Save' and watch the file float to the lower right hand corner drop box, the cursor on the screen blinking an entreaty. Blinking for me to click open the ominous new message from Daphne Winthrop.

To: DRyan@halyarcapitolinvsec.co
From: dwinthrop_vp@publicrelations.info
Subject: I don't know what to say

Dexter. To say I was surprised to get your message is an understatement... Excited and surprised. After seeing StarGate the other weekend, I was sure you were going to ask me on a date until your Aunt interrupted... and I was disappointed you asked me to Grace's engagement party as your Fake Date. I would have absolutely been proud to go as your official date. I think you're charming and disarming, and since we're being direct—very handsome. So yes. Yes! I would love to go on a date with you. I've been waiting for you to ask since the movie theater. Here is my cell phone number again just in case you lost it: 298-555.9392 Well, better get back to work! LOL.

Talk to you soon, I hope.

Daphne

To: dwinthrop_vp@publicrelations.info
From: DRyan@halyarcapitolinvsec.co
Subject: Confession time.

Dear Daphne,

I have a confession to make since we're being honest and it's easier for me to hide behind technology. Alright, here it is: my sisters wrote that first message behind my back and I found the email by accident, and I was furious. But now? I'm glad. As horrible and stupid as their message made me sound, and as embarrassed as I am that they did it, I'm glad.

DPR

To: DRyan@halyarcapitolinvsec.co
From: dwinthrop_vp@publicrelations.info
Subject: Me too.

Dexter, I should have guessed that you didn't write that first note. I guess I was so excited to receive it that... it didn't occur to me that you wouldn't use words like "Lame" and "Geek" in an email to describe yourself, because you are NEITHER of those things. LOL! Oh lord,

you must have died when you saw their note. What a couple of beasts! You're right though. I'm glad they did it because... when would you have gotten around to telling me how you felt? I'd be old and gray by then!
Daphne

To: dwinthrop_vp@publicrelations.info
From: DRyan@halyarcapitolinvsec.co
Subject: You'd be waiting a long time

Dear Daphne,

Honestly? I'm not surprised by them messaging you; they've been doing stuff like this since they were old enough to understand what a prank was. But that doesn't mean I didn't want to *kill* them. When I found the message "I" sent you, I couldn't even read through the whole thing—I could only see red. I mean—what made them think I'd call myself lame? But enough about me; do you have any brothers/sisters that drive you insane?
DPR

To: DRyan@halyarcapitolinvsec.co
From: dwinthrop_vp@publicrelations.info
Subject: Not a Lonely Only

Dexter, Fortunately and Unfortunately, I have a sister although my mom says sometimes my Dad acts like a small child, so it's like having three kids. Haha. Growing up, I always wish I had a twin. I think your sisters are badass— I'm totally digging their Twin Voodoo and am kind of jealous, not gonna lie.

They're so pretty and cute for evil masterminds.

So… got anything planned for the weekend? Did you see the commercial on the Sci-Fi channel for the Star Trek Comic Con thing?

Daphne

To: dwinthrop_vp@publicrelations.info
From: DRyan@halyarcapitolinvsec.co
Subject: Me finally asking you

Dear Daphne,

I don't usually go to Comic Con events… I'm more of a laid back, lazy poster yielding nerd. I don't get all crazy and I don't have any collectible figurines still in the boxes, LOL; fine. A few. But yeah. I did see that commercial but that's the twins' family birthday with the whole Ryan side of the family. Grace, Elliot—the whole crazy clan. Are you brave enough? Would you have any interest in going? It's this Sunday around three.

Eleven

Daphne: *Okay, just to clarify... am I going with you this weekend to your sisters' party as a [fill in blank]?*
Dexter: *Date?*
Daphne: *Yes. I'm sorry to ask and I know it's awkward but it will drive me crazy not knowing. But we did go on that FAKE date... so this one is... [fill in blank]?*
Dexter: *Not fake. This is me—for once in my life—sucking it up and putting myself out there; Yeah. I'd like it to be a date. How does two o'clock sound?*
Daphne: *I would love that. Two o'clock.*
Dexter: *It's a date.*

Daphne: *Hey, it's me. Do you think your mom needs me to bring anything this weekend for the party? Like fruit or something...?*
Dexter: *No, don't worry about it. She'll have enough*

food there to feed a small herd of elephants. Or assholes.

Daphne: *:) Truth? I only asked you that as an excuse to text you. Is that weird?*

Dexter: *No weirder than you showing up to bake cookies at my mom's house...*

Daphne: *Oh god! Please don't remind me. Tabitha told me that was a horrible idea; I should have listened, but awkwardly... I was already in your mom's apron.*

Dexter: *Truth? I think I dreamt about that apron.*

Dexter: *Is that weird?*

Daphne: *Maybe someone else might think so, but I don't. LOL.*

Dexter: *I hope you don't think I'm being too forward, but I bought the twins a gift and signed your name to their card... I figured, since they already think we're dating, it would be okay.*

Daphne: *You are so sweet. Yes. That's absolutely okay.*

Daphne: *Shoot. I have a meeting in three minutes. Better get moving. Talk later?*

Daphne: *I'm back. Curious about what gift we're giving the twins?*

Dexter: *A spy kit.*

Twelve

Daphne

The twins love their spy kit.

Fully equipped with magnifying glass, finger printing kit, and baggies to store collected evidence, the cheap child's spy kit has the sisters bent at the waist, laughing hysterically. Before moving on to open their next gift, Lucy removes the kit's rubber gloves, snaps them at the wrist, and asks the family members crowded around the room who wants to be their first victim.

Half the room laughs uproariously; their Uncle Derek throws his arms up, demanding to be finger printed.

"Now maybe they'll leave me alone," Dexter gripes beside me as we stand in the threshold of the living room, watching the twins rip through the rest of their gifts like seven-year-old kids. "Even if the kit is just a toy, look at how happy they are."

"You know what I always wanted growing up?" I muse. "A metal detector; a real one—not one of those cheap, crappy ones."

Dexter laughs. "Me too! Imagine all the shit we'd find. Coins, jewelry."

"Pirate's booty, for sure," I tease. "Sunken treasure."

"Oh, now we're taking this metal detector in the ocean? Shit, I was thinking just parks and the beach. The ocean opens up a whole world of possibilities. What body of water would we explore first?"

I tap my chin, pretending to think. "I've actually given this some thought. It would definitely need to be somewhere near Spain."

"Okay Magellan." Dexter's burst of surprise is loud and raucous. "Why Spain?"

I roll my eyes, and give him a smirk of superiority. "All the shipwrecks from the explorers crossing over? Sheesh."

He's not convinced. "But aren't the best places to scuba dive in the Caribbean?"

My head gives a little shake. "No, no, no—I'm not talking about scuba diving; that's all surface stuff. We'd need to dive down deep—"

"—What the hell are you yammering on about over here? All I heard was *blah blah I'm a giant nerd who gave my sisters a spy kit*."

I inwardly groan, pivoting on my heel at the interruption.

Elliot. Of course.

He holds a beer towards Dexter as an offering.

My date takes it, hesitantly, his demeanor going from flirty and fun to guarded in a matter of nanoseconds.

My lips clamp shut, pursing with displeasure; not at the interruption, but at the rude way he went about it. Good lord, didn't his mother teach him any manners? You don't walk over and insult someone. I glance over at his mother, Aunt Tory, who sits perched daintily on the couch, sipping out of a champagne glass. Coiffed, strikingly made-up to the nines and discernibly high-maintenance, I acknowledge that she doesn't *look* like she's spent Elliot's childhood years teaching him modesty.

I also acknowledge that perhaps he doesn't know any better, and allow him some leeway. After all, the guy probably can't help himself.

He was raised this way.

"Hey Elliot," I start. "It's good to see you again."

Lie #1.

"Right? It's nice not to have the huge crowd we had at Gracie's party—now we can actually talk without all the music and annoying dancing," he schmoozes. The charming smile doesn't reach his calculating brown eyes.

"Oh, totally," I agree. *Lie #2.*

Elliot moves closer, his elbow giving Dexter an almost unperceivable nudge, jostling my date towards the wall. Away from me.

My green eyes become slits. This guy is certifiable.

"What are you doing after this?" He wonders aloud, blatantly ignoring his cousin. "It's a Sunday night but we should still do something."

"What a great suggestion; we should." *Just not with you, asshole.* "Dexter sweetie, let's do something after this."

The patronizing bastard scoffs. "Come on now, get real. You don't think I know what's going on here?"

My mouth falls open—actually falls open at his audacity—the anger inside me beginning its slow roll up my throat, past my lips. My claws come out. "Wow. Just... *wow*. You know something pal, you are seriously one shitty—"

"Cousin!" The twins announce, appearing out of nowhere, their lithe arms going around Elliot's shoulders. For once, their timing is impeccable.

Amelia gives her brother a quick peck on the cheek. "Dex, mom wants you to run upstairs and grab that picture of you and Dad from the Vacation from Hell of 2010. You know the one—where Lucy and I are both crying in the background—"

"—and you and Dad are smiling at the camera—"

"—and Mom looks like she's about to lose her mind—" Amelia giggles.

"—She says it's in your closet." Lucy finishes.

"Daphne, you should definitely go with him," they say together, grinning their identical grins. Their eyes are wide. Calculating.

They know exactly what's going on and suddenly... I adore them. I adore these perfect, weird, sassy human beings.

"So, this is your childhood bedroom, huh? The room you grew up in? I didn't get a tour when I was here baking cookies with your sisters."

"Yup, this was my room for eighteen years. Where all the magic *didn't* happen."

Yeah, it's not exactly a babe magnet: shocking blue stripped wallpaper with an orange basketball border. Vintage Sci-Fi poster of 3,000 Leagues Under the Sea. A poster of Doctor Zvago. Academic Decathlon trophies shining on an oak shelf. His High School diploma and medals hanging from blue and red ribbons.

It's sparse; clean. Slightly juvenile—but then again, it *is* the room from his childhood.

"Give me a minute to find the picture my Mom wanted, okay? Sit tight. I know it's in here somewhere..." Dexter disappears into the closet, and the sound of shoes, totes and clutter being shifted ensues. *"Shit, there used to be a box in here with..."* Clatter. Bang. *"Where the hell is it..."*

His muffled voice fades in and out of the walk-in closet, where I hear the distinct sound of a box being pulled open as he hunts for this elusive, lost photograph. I wander to the far side of the room, trailing a hand lightly over the Star Wars comforter laid out over the twin bed, my fingertips gliding along the course cotton fabric.

Darth Vader occupies the entire bed.

"I wonder why your mom hasn't redecorated in here. You've been moved out how long?" I ponder out loud, more to myself than anyone else.

His voice filters into the room from the deep pit of his closet, loud enough to be heard over the chatter and laughter of his rambunctious family floating up the stairs and through the vents in the floorboards.

"Uh, I moved out eight years ago?" Dexter sticks his head out, peering at me from behind the doorjamb, holding a tiny action figure towards me. "Hey, I know I said I didn't have many of these, but check this out! I totally forgot about this collection! I wonder where the rest of them are…"

I bounce on the bed, excited, extending my arms to take it. "Whoa! You have a Battlestar Galactica Cylon Centurion action figure! Where did you get that?"

He holds it towards me, faltering mid-step. "Wait. You actually *know* what this is?"

He looks suitably impressed.

I roll my eyes. "Dexter. I was at StarGate alone on a Saturday night—of course I know what a Cylon Centurion is." I grab at it, turning it this-way-and-that to examine it. "In perfect condition, too."

Dexter pauses in the doorway of the closet, pupils dilating, the figurine all but forgotten as he watches me, eyes blazing. "Shit Daphne, you're kind of turning me on right now with all this geek talk."

"Is that so?" I lean back on his pillows, channeling my inner Tabitha, the Cylon still in my hand. "In that case… Did you know the starship that became the Blockade Runner in *Star Wars: Episode four* was the original design for the Millennium Falcon?"

His nostrils flare and he takes a step closer.

I press on, willing him towards me. "Did you know," I start slowly. Very slowly, each word pronounced barely above a whisper. "That they still haven't named Yoda's species?"

Oh my god, where is all this random trivia coming from?

Dexter removes his glasses, setting them on a nearby dresser. Unwavering, the brown irises practically sizzle as he focuses every iota of his attention on me.

I stare *holes* into those glasses.

"Can you see without those?" I tease quietly as he

stalks forward.

He chuckles then, the sound low and deep against the silence of the bedroom. My teeth bite down on my lower lip to hide a shy smile. "*Can* you?"

His moves closer, closer still. "I see *you*, if that's what you mean."

Swallowing my nerves, I murmur, "Did you know..."

"Did I know what? Talk nerdy to me, Daphne." He falls to the carpet, on his knees between my legs, running his hands up the length of my thighs. "Don't stop."

Up and down, up and down my thighs his palms go.

"D-did you k-know," I gulp when he leans in, his delicious lips consuming the pulse in my neck. My heart beats wildly outside of my chest, and I struggle to catch my breath. "Throughout the course of the Battlestar Galactica series, Sheba never fires her laser pistol. Not even once."

"Actually, I *did* know that." Dexter's nose skims idly up the column of my neck, his lips trailing along behind.

"You're such a geek." I breathe.

"So are you." Up and down, up and down my thighs his palms leisurely go.

"Dexter, what are you waiting for?"

A pause. "I don't know."

A sigh. "Stop thinking and *just do it*."

"Know what? Call me a glutton for punishment, but I kind of want..." The question purrs next to my ear. "I kind of want to hear you say it."

That I can do.

With a tiny nod and a tilted neck, I whisper into the room, "Kiss me."

Kiss me.

He does.

Large hands cupping my face, Dexter's thumbs tenderly stroke my cheekbones before he lowers his mouth. Our lips connect with the very barest of contact before touching, a veritable shockwave ricocheting to every nerve ending in my body; like a tiny voltage of electricity.

Every cell tingles, every nerve quivers—and all we're doing is kissing.

Softly at first, our kisses are small exploratory ones. Small yes, but bound to leave imprint after imprint on my heart.

I hesitate, pulling back; wanting to remember this moment forever, certain that *this* will be my last first kiss.

Dexter's brows furrow, concerned, drawing his hands away. "What's wrong?"

I grab them, holding them steady. Holding them on my flesh, not wanting to lose the connection.

"Nothing's wrong," I murmur. "Everything is *right*."

The mattress dips when I lean in towards him, settling my lips back on Dexter's mouth.

His lips part.

Our tongues tentatively meet in a painfully slow dance.

It's tender. It's sexy.

It's torture.

Our lips press harder, tongues searching. Urgently now.

"Oh my god," Dexter moans into me. "It feels so fucking good kissing you." His fingers tangle their way into my hair, running through the strands before cupping the back of my neck in his large palm. "I could kiss you forever."

"Yes please," I manage to whimper into his warm, open mouth. Tongues tangle, wet and delicious and positively intoxicating.

A labored groan. "Shit, we shouldn't have started this."

"Why?"

A deep, virile growl. "Because I won't want to stop."

"Then we won't."

"Daphne..." His lithe fingers *toy* with the tiny pearl button at the collar of my demure cotton shirt—the one I wore specifically to impress his grandmother—plucking at it but leaving it intact. Ugh, the *tease*. "My grandparents are downstairs in the..."

His voice falters when I reach between us, running my index and middle finger inside the waistband of his jeans; up the front of his rigged zipper, grasping somewhat desperately for the outline of his—

"You're right, you're right," I chant. "We need to stop."

"We need to stop," he repeats with determination, his breathing arduous; a pearl button slides free. Then another. Then, "Stop me, Daphne."

He tongue dampens my neck, sucking gently.

Now we're both moaning.

Mmmm.

"Oh god Dexter, *I can't*, I can't, your hands feel *too* good."

Breathing heavy, and with one last kiss to my temple, he releases me to stand. Pushing from his knees to a stand, he backs away, his fingers flex and immediately fly to run through his hair; sexual tension crackling through the air with rapid alacrity.

Without meaning to, my eyes shoot to the bulge between his thighs—to his glaringly obvious arousal.

My girly parts whimper in dismay.

I stand too, pressing my fingers against my swollen lips; they're raw and painfully tender and wonderful. I give them a few light swipes as if to quell the pain before holding out my trembling hands.

"Look at me; I'm shaking."

A second ticks by.

Then another.

Then another.

Then…

"Ah, *fuck it*."

We crash feverishly into each other then, my back hitting the blue wallpapered wall, shaking a nearby shelf. I don't know who's tugging the hem of my shirt free from the waistband of my jeans—his grasping hands or mine or both—but together, we frantically free all the buttons until my shirt's pulled open.

Finally, blessedly ripped open.

I moan in relief when Dexter connects with my bare skin. The tips of his fingers travel up my bare stomach, his palms a tense, restrained caress against my flesh.

Over my bra. Over the swell of my breasts.

My body strains up to meet his touch.

His head dips. He reaches down, grabs my ass in both his palms and hauls me to the dresser.

Lips. Teeth. Skin.

Tongue.

"I'm a horrible person," I gasp. "This is so wrong—your grandmother is downstairs."

He stifles my protests with his mouth, his sexy, *smart*,

skillful mouth… we can't get our tongues deep enough as he lifts me with a grunt, knocking a lamp to the carpeted floor with a loud thump and sitting me in the center of his dresser.

The light bulb hits the ground and shatters.

He rocks his hips into me, pounding the dresser into the drywall as we paw at each other, rattling the framed High School diploma hanging above the Debate team medals that jingle and sway on their hooks.

We don't notice.

We don't care.

He feels so good, he feels so good, he feels so—

Thirteen

Daphne

"Uh, Daphne *might* want to put her shirt back on. Just sayin—"

"—And fix her hair."

The twins stand in the open doorway of Dexter's old room, identical expressions fixated on us, unreadable. Completely pokerfaced—as if they hadn't just walked in on Dexter and I in the middle of us dry humping against the wall and tearing at each other's clothes. As if my shirt wasn't open and my breasts weren't threatening to spill out of my bra.

Like this kind of thing casually happens every Saturday.

I fumble blindly for the buttons on my shirt, fitting each tiny pearl through its hole, mindlessly shoving them through, desperate to match them up but not taking the time to actually do it properly.

I need to get my breasts covered.

The twins saunter a little farther into Dexter's room, past the dresser I'm perched on to study the spines of his collection of high school yearbooks.

"Mom sent us looking for you, F-Y-I, so don't get your boxers in a twist. You know the drill: we can't light the candles or sing Happy Birthday until everyone is—"

"—Present and accounted for," the twins parrot, prattling on as if nothing was amiss.

"And since they think you've been MIA for the past…"

Amelia checks the time on her phone.

"Twenty minutes."

"—Even though *everyone* heard the loud banging coming from up here." Lucy crosses her arms and purses her lips. "What the heck did you think you were doing?"

Amelia snorts. "You should know better than this Dex, going at it in *this* house? Remember how thin the walls are? You can't even—"

"—Whisper without someone hearing it through the vents."

They stare at us, Amelia raising her eyebrows and Lucy tapping her foot on the carpeted floor.

"Well?"

"Are you coming downstairs or what?"

Dexter and I stare after them as they airily saunter back out into the hallway, not a care in the world. And that thing I said before about *adoring* them?

Yeah.

Forget I mentioned it.

Dexter

Things go from bad to worse when we descend the stairs, my cousin Elliot waiting at the bottom, hand wrapped around the finial post of the wooden rail.

He starts in as soon as the twins usher Daphne into the kitchen, out of earshot.

"Jesus fucking Christ, Dexter." Elliot hisses, grabbing my arm the second I round the staircase in the foyer. He strong-arms me through the hall, cornering me near my dad's office. "Were you *seriously* fucking your hot girlfriend with a party going on?"

I register *hot* and *girlfriend*, cataloging them in my brain for future use. Aggravated, I give him a glower.

"Why would you even ask me that?"

Elliot claps a hand on my shoulder, emitting a low whistle. I shrug him off. "Several reasons. One: she looks thoroughly *fucked*. Or drunk, and Aunt Georgia isn't serving alcohol. So which is it?"

"Would you please stop using the word fuck when you're talking about Daphne?"

Elliot crosses his arms, pleased with himself. "Two: I notice you aren't denying fucking her."

I shake my head, pushing away from the wall, willing him to walk away.

He doesn't comply. "Three: *everyone* heard the

moaning. I'll admit, it was pretty hot and I was getting off on it until your Dad cranked the stereo and your mom did that weird laugh thing she does when she's about to lose her shit."

My back turned to him, I walk towards the kitchen leaving him trailing after me. "We weren't having sex in my room so shut the fuck up about it."

He's skeptical. "Well then you should have. Christ, man up, dude. Your girlfriend is a hot piece of ass. What she sees in you is—"

"—None of your business, you douchenozzle." An agitated feminine voice interrupts from behind, startling us both. I expect to find Daphne coming to my defense when I spin on my heel, but instead I find…

The twins.

Great. More drama; just what I need.

"You're being a real dickshitter," Lucy scowls. "Why are you always such an ass?"

Elliot's eyes bug out of his head at their foul language. I mean—all dressed up in their conservative birthday dresses, they hardly look like the truckers they're beginning to sound like.

"What the hell Dex—are you going to let her—them—talk to me like that?"

The twins cross their arms and Amelia *hmphs*. "Are you even listening to yourself?"

Lucy laughs. "All we need to do is go back in the kitchen and tell Aunt Tory you're—"

"—In here using profanity and talking shit about Daphne." Amelia's own use of profanity is not lost on me.

"Maligning her."

The girls nod. "If you scare her off after we worked

so hard to get her here…"

Lucy makes a slicing gesture across her neck with her hand: *dead*.

"Wait. How do you know the word malign?" Sorry, I can't help asking.

"Maligning?" The twins cross their arms and roll their narrowed eyes, speaking at the same time. "AP English."

"What's AP English?" Elliot probes.

More eye rolling. "Advanced Placement."

This gives me pause. Because, "If you're in AP English, why'd you write such a shitty letter to Daphne when you hijacked my email—you know what? Never mind. I don't want to know. Jesus you two, please just go back to your party."

Both my sisters stand tall, unflinching. "We'll wait here while you finish him off." Lucy gives her chin an encouraging nod in Elliot's direction.

Finish him off? "Okay tiny Godfathers, bring it down a notch. This isn't the mob."

Elliot glances at me with disbelief still etched across his brow. And pity. "Shit man, are they always like this?"

I chuckle, smacking my cousin on the back and moving him towards the party. "Unfortunately, yeah."

God, I really do love those two.

Crazy little weirdos.

Daphne

"So, this is me."

"Yup, this is you." Dexter taps on the steering wheel with his palm, glancing out the window up at my condo. My little front porch light glows in the dark, illuminating my dark gray front door and the adorable painted snowman leaning up against the brick wall. The light also bounces off the lenses of his glasses, making it hard to read his expression.

Pulling his car neatly into a parking spot in front of my awning, I unbuckle my seatbelt but make no move to exit the vehicle when he shifts into park.

The engine idles.

The radio is silent.

"Are you sure you don't want to go do something? It's still pretty early."

Nine o'clock on the dot on a Sunday night.

"Don't feel obligated to continue this farce of an evening." His chuckle is sardonic and patronizing. "Although I do appreciate the sentiment."

Farce? Obligated?

"Obligated? I thought this was a date."

Dexter laughs again, pushing his sexy tortoiseshell glasses up the bridge of his nose. The buttoned up collared shirt beneath his winter jacket peeks through, and my eyes travel of the column of his neck to his strong jaw line.

The place where I want to put my lips.

"Dexter, if Elliot said something to upset you, I—"

"—Let me stop you right there." He twists his body to face me from the driver's seat. "Nothing—and I mean nothing—Elliot says upsets me; it's the fact that he *says* anything at all and there's nothing I can do about it. He's not some guy off the street. He's family. So as much as I want to smash his face in, I can't. Because my freaking grandmother is usually in the other room."

He's pissed off and agitated and *passionate*.

"Elliot's always been like this, and thank god it's not just with me. He's a dick to our cousin John, too, and Little Erik who's what—ten years younger than him? What an ass. You don't do that shit to a kid." He lets out a puff of frustration. "Anyway. I'd love to deck him, but I never will, and that's the pisser of it."

Ass. Punch. Dick. Deck. *Pisser*.

Oh my god, why is this turning me on?

There's something wrong with me, I know it. Maybe it's been too long since I've had sex and I'm going through some kind of withdrawal, where mundane words trigger dirty, dirty thoughts.

I watch words and sentences come out of Dexter's beautifully sculpted lips, but I stop hearing them all, so lost in thought. So lost in the thought of him taking me inside and—

My head tips to the side and I study him.

I look up.

"What's... that *look?*"

Crap, he's studying me now, too, but his look isn't one of desire. It's one of confusion.

I know, I know, it's shameful! But he's so kind and patient and sweet and handsome and I like him and I want... everything. I want everything with him.

I need to know if he wants it too, but...

Guh!

"Why don't I walk you to the door."

Of its own volition, my head gives a nod.

Grabbing my purse from the backseat of his Audi while he jogs around to open the passenger side door, I step out, one leg after the next. Put one foot in front of the other as we walk unhurriedly to the front door.

Keys in hand, they jingle in the silent night, but I make no move to fit them into the lock, just like Dexter makes no move to kiss me. In fact, rather than move closer, his hands disappear into the pockets of his navy pea coat, stuffed inside protectively. Whether it's against me, or the cold, frigid air, is beyond me.

"Thanks for inviting me along today, despite all the crazy." A smile tips my lips. "Your sisters are really something. Do you even realize how much they love you?"

"Of course I know how much they love me. They have to; I'm their brother."

"No, I mean—they really love you. They set this whole thing up; getting me to your mom's house to bake cookies so I'd be thrust in your path. Emailing me from your phone. Breaking up the tension with Elliot and threatening to cut a bitch." This earns me a low chuckle. "You are their everything. It's..."

"I haven't thought of it that way. They're such pains in my ass most of the time it's easy to lose sight behind their intentions."

"I bet. But truly—they adore you." My hand finds the

sleeve of his thick, wool coat, and I squeeze, relishing the feel of him under my gloved hand. "*I* adore you, Dexter."

With a nervous blush that has nothing to do with the cold, I glance from under my long lashes into his brown eyes and wait for his reaction.

Pleasure curves his mouth. "You do?"

"I do."

He hums. "That's good because I adore *you*."

"You do?"

His head dips. "Yeah."

Beneath the awning of my tiny condo, under the winter stars, our lips touch for the second time tonight. And when he finally digs his hands out of his pockets, our fingers lace together.

I shiver.

"You need to get inside," he murmurs at the corner of my mouth. "It's freezing."

"Dexter," I breath, a tad wistful. "Come inside with me."

My key goes in the lock. Feet hit the tiled foyer; shoes get kicked off. Large hands find the base of my neck, pulling me in hungrily and pushing my back against the wall in the entryway.

"I really *do* want to talk and get to know you, I swear I do." He breaths into my hair. "But all I can think about right now is—"

"—Ripping all my clothes off and—"

"—hauling you to the bedroom."

Oh jeez, we're doing our own version of the Twin Speak thing, finishing each other's sentences, the words flowing out our mouths as our lips and bodies collide. My hands fist the collar of his coat, seeking out the row of toggles barring me from unbuttoning his dress shirt.

Dexter sheds his coat, thank god; it drops to the floor in a heap, followed by his knit hat, gloves and—only Dexter would remove his socks.

Grinning like a fool I shuck my own coat, hat and gloves, adding them to the pile on the floor.

Leading Dexter up the stairs and down the narrow hallway to my bedroom, I turn to face him once we're through the threshold of my door. Instead of a hurried frenzy to tear at each other's clothes, we face each other, drinking each other in from head to toe. Admiring each other.

Reveling in each other.

My chest swells with complete happiness when Dexter's hand gently cups my cheek, his fingers stroking my jaw line as he watches me, one part captivated—the other part aroused.

My eyes flutter shut when he leans in to land a kiss to the corner of my lips. The curve of my cheekbones. My eyelids.

Pleasure sends a ripple of tingles surging throughout my body, tipping my head back, giving him the access he needs to—

Gently suck on my neck.

His tongue slides leisurely along the column of my throat until his nose is buried in the hair behind my ear. A moan escapes my lips as our breathing becomes labored—I swear we're both panting; but is that his breath or mine?

Our tongues are sliding together when our bodies finally meet; my body sighs in relief. Exhales. Vibrates on high with anticipation.

"I love these glasses," I slur, finger tracing the frame at his temple, back-and-forth...then back again.

"What?" Dexter sounds as drunk as I feel.

"Your glasses, your glasses, God I love your glasses."

"You don't say?" More kisses against my neck. "That's got to be a first."

His ministrations on my body feel so good I can barely roll my eyes. "S-somehow, I doubt that. *Mmm...* you would be surprised at how... *your tongue feels so good...* many women find glasses and bowties and suspenders sexy."

"I only need *one* woman to find it sexy."

"I do, I do," I chant, finally groaning into his mouth when our mouths meet; finally, blessedly meet.

"Take them off me," he demands.

So I do.

I do; and he's gorgeous.

Fourteen

Dexter

Holy shit.

Daphne Winthrop is taking off my shirt.

Tugging the hem from the waistband of my dark jeans… hands splayed on my smooth chest, her soft palms running over my abs and pec muscles. Fingers trace my hardening nipples.

I bite down on my lower lip, nostrils flaring. At my sides, I clench and unclench my fists. The desire to wrap my hands around her waist is unbearable when she finally pushes the dress shirt down over my shoulders, down my arms, down to the floor.

Daphne Winthrop is taking off my pants.

Belt.

Then, before I can wrap my brain around it, the snap on my fly is popped open, the zipper slowly being tugged down. So slowly the simple sound of the metal track coming undone has my dick throbbing painfully hard.

Anticipation pulses through my veins, every fantasy I've ever had can't beat this reality as my pants get pushed down around my ankles.

I step out of them, and am slowly propelled towards the bed in nothing but my boxer briefs. My legs hit the mattress as she propels me back, back, back.

"Lay down against the headboard?" comes her quiet request. "I want you to watch me undress. Is that okay?"

Somehow, I manage to nod.

Swallow air.

Breathe Dexter, I remind myself. Breathe.

Holy shit. Daphne Winthrop is about to strip all the clothes off her gorgeous body and get naked.

For me.

She starts at the top button of her collared shirt, plucking one free from the hole, then another.

One.

Two.

My eyes are riveted to that gap of exposed skin; fucking riveted as a third button is plucked free, followed by a fourth. Her hands pause momentarily to part the seam of her shirt, the creamy expanse of cleavage sacredly, beatifically—*oh shit*—full. I've heard the phrase "spilling over" a few times, but I've never seen boobs overflowing a bra in person.

I force my face to remain impassive; willing my jaw to stay closed.

Instead of unbuttoning the rest of her pretty, preppy shirt, her hands glide to the waistband of her jeans. The snap on her fly opens; zipper forced down. I watch as her hands drift over her pale, perfect skin and push the denim down over her slim hips.

White lace boy shorts.

Flawless porcelain skin.

Daphne steps out of her skinny jeans, leaving them on the carpet in a heap, and strides slowly forward, fingers poised on the fifth button of her shirt as she comes to stand next to the bed.

With baited breath, I wait.

Daphne

He can't take his eyes off me, and quite honestly, he's holding so still I'm afraid he's stopped breathing. Dexter is completely... motionless. Crap. What if the sight of my near naked boobs gave the guy a stroke?

I pause, waiting to unbutton number five. "Dexter?"

His mumbled, incoherent, "Huh?" puts a coy smile on my lips, giving me leave to continue my strip tease.

Climbing up onto the bed, I crawl towards him in the center of the mattress and note with satisfaction his nostrils flaring when I straddle his hips. Dexter's hungry eyes roam my body as I pull off my pale pink shirt, dragging it slowly down my arms. Unceremoniously, I toss it on the ground next to the bed.

"*Oh shit,*" he groans when I reach back and unclasp my bra; it joins my shirt and jeans in a pile on the floor.

Only underwear separates us now.

I lean forward, my breasts rubbing against his chest, the sound of his gravelly groan and my moan filling the air. My hands roam his smooth pecs; Dexter is toned perfection. Olive skin that's sinewy and trim and hard with perfect nipples. I run my trembling hands over them now, fingering one in a leisurely... burning... tease.

Beneath me, his hips give a jerk, and I rotate my pelvis onto his straining erection; it's just *begging* for attention.

Begging.

Begging and hard and rubbing so painfully good against my center that a stifling whimper gets caught in my throat as Dexter finally leans forward to capture my lips with his.

Suddenly, I'm on my back, his mouth and tongue are everywhere.

My neck.

My collarbone.

My breasts.

Oh god, my breasts. I arch my back into his mouth as he *sucks and licks and squeezes*, the pressure building between my legs so agonizing that when I pull his hair, we both gasp out in pleasure.

"You are going to drive me out of my damn fucking mind," he rasps, grinding and grinding his dick into the apex of my thighs, his head still bent at my breasts. His large hand cups one, squeezing gently. "Jesus Christ you feel so good."

I glance down between our bodies at our pelvises pressed together, feeling my eyes glaze over with arousal. Excitement. Wanting to *feel* him, I find the elastic waistband of his boxers, my fingers trailing along the edge before going under. Inside.

Grasping the hard, rigid length of him.

Stroking him up and down as he whimpers and moans into my mouth; it's a low, tortured guttural sound that has me desperately pushing his underwear down his hips, my palms smoothing over his firm backside.

Dexter flexes as I squeeze and knead, pulling him down into me by the ass cheeks, eventually, he kicks off the offensive boxers.

"Get on your back," I whisper when he's scrumptiously naked.

I start at his neck, languidly lavishing kisses along the pulse beating erratically in his throat—his heart. Kiss his stomach, lick his abs, his belly button and below…

I suck.

And swirl.

And suck.

"*Oh fuck, oh f-fuck,*" he chants, clutching the bedspread with a vice grip in his fantastically large palms. "*Fuck, oh fuck.*"

He's babbling and grimacing in agony and it's glorious. His dirty cursing only serves to make my lady parts tingle. Ache.

"*Shit…stop, baby, I want to fuck you… stop, Daphne … don't stop. Oh…f-fuck.*"

He comes, his head falling back against the pillow.

Dexter

"You're so beautiful," I murmur into her ear, my cock already hard again. "So beautiful."

I can't even believe this shit is real; that I'm in her bed and she's spread out next to me, my hand roaming her smooth, naked skin.

And that she's letting me.

Or that she's encouraging me.

My dick has literally *never* been in a girl's mouth.

And Daphne Winthrop *blew* me.

On purpose.

Speaking of which… her hand clasps mine, dragging it down under the covers and onto her right breast; I begin a slow caress with my thumb that has her throwing her head back on the pillow and breathlessly saying my name.

Not gonna lie: I push the bedspread down so I can watch my hand stroke her boobs. They're full and round in my palm, her nipples pink and perfect. Obviously watching myself fondle her tits makes my dick throb; I'm starring in my own goddamn sexual fantasies for Christ sake.

"*You're* beautiful." Her hand is on my inner thigh, then my pulsating cock, as she whispers in my ear. Licks it. "Everything about you turns me on."

"Daphne, I can't believe I'm about to say this, but…" Shit. Fuck. Damn. "I… don't have a condom."

Her hand grazes my cheek. "It's okay, baby. I do, I do. I mean… it's a *hundred* years old, but… I'm also on the pill so…"

Within moments the package is being ripped open, the condom is on and I'm sliding home, the only coherent thoughts after that?

If I died right now, I'd already be in heaven.

Daphne

"I love Star Wars," I slur as he rotates his hips—pressing me harder against the wall, his hands gripping my ass and squeezing. "I love it."

"Oh yeah?" Grunt. Pant. Groan.

"*Yes*, oh…oh! Yes." My toes curl.

"Fuck yeah you love Star Wars," Dexter moans as he grinds and grinds those lean, sexy hips, his hand gripping my backside. Gripping my ass. "Uh… god… fu-ck*kk*…"

"Dexter, *oh god*, mmm*nuh*…."

"Daphne, baby," his voice is strained. "I could live inside you."

"*Yes*," I beg. "Yes, please."

Yes.

Yes.

Yes.

Tabitha: *So. "Baking cookies" is your new code word for sex?*

Me: *Yeah, pretty much. Dexter is… I don't even have the words.*

Tabitha: *I believe the phrase you're searching for is*

"Orgasmic."

Me: *You're not allowed to say shit like that. Only I am.*

Tabitha: *Le'sigh. Fine. But I'm using your story in a book; sorry, I won't be able to help myself...*

Me: *I'd argue with you but I know it would be pointless. At least make my character gorgeous and smart and hilarious.*

Tabitha: *You just described yourself ;)*

Me: *Aww, that's why I love you so much.*

Tabitha: *So this thing with Dexter... can you see it getting serious?*

Me: *Oh gosh—YES! Yes, he's... awesome. LOL. Just the thought of him has me...*

Tabitha: *Wanting to "bake cookies?"*

Me: *Dozens and dozens of cookies...*

Epilogue

Daphne

Six or 8 months later…who really knows?

"I wonder what the occasion is," I mumble to a beautiful, blonde haired Greyson in the kitchen of her brother Collin's new condo. His second condo in a year, but… somehow this doesn't feel like a house warming party. "What's up with this little shin-dig they decided to throw last minute?"

He and Tabitha have been living together for the past six months—dating for eight—and tonight they're throwing an impromptu…whatever this party is.

"Well," she says conspiratorially, giving me a nudge and grabbing a handful of chips. "*My* theory is that they're going to announce an engagement. At least, I *hope* that's what this is. They can't keep having these house warming parties."

I glance around at the room full of people; Tabitha's parents. Collin and Greyson's parents. Greyson and her rugged, rugby playing boyfriend Calvin. More family. More friends. A crowded room gathered in Tab and Collin's spacious high-rise condo.

"Or maybe this is about one of her books?" I speculate. Tabitha is an author, and she's on book number three. "Maybe she's made a best seller list somewhere?"

Greyson doesn't look convinced. "Maybe. But I'm still putting my money on an engagement. Do you see the way my brother is following her around, waiting on her hand and foot?"

I had noticed that. Collin fetching her water. Rubbing her shoulders while she spoke to her parents. Bringing her little plates of food. Touching her.

Hmmm.

I'm not convinced this is them springing an engagement on us. That's not Tabitha's style. "Maybe, but they haven't even been together for a year."

Collin's sister looks at me, incredulously. "Those two? Are you kidding me? They were crazy about each other from day one. Almost inseparable."

I scrunch my face. "I think you're remembering it wrong. Collin harassed her, embarrassed her, and she spent *how* many weeks avoiding him. When you say 'crazy about each other,' you're thinking of you and Calvin."

Greyson and her boyfriend are in crazy, mad, love with each other, and have been since the day they met; the day she created a fake boyfriend named Cal Thompson to keep her nosy friends off her back.

Almost the same way Dexter had asked me to be his fake girlfriend for one night so his family wouldn't meddle in his love life.

Actually, come to think of it, all three of us—Greyson, Tabitha and I—lied at the beginning of our relationships; Greyson lied about inventing a fake boyfriend, Tabitha lied about being an author and hid her books from everyone, and I lied about being Dexter's girlfriend.

What pretty little liars we all turned out to be; thank god everything ended well for us.

"Having a good time?" I ask, sidling up to Dexter. He slides a hand around my waist, pulling me in. Pulling me close and planting a quick kiss on my neck, just under my ear; my favorite spot.

I shiver every time.

"I'm having a good time; I just wish Collin hadn't invited my sisters. Why would he do that? They're driving me crazy. I mean—just look at them over there." He nods to the opposite side of the room to where the twins are holding court, gesturing wildly and laughing uproariously.

I have a sneaking suspicion they're re-enacting the moment they came to Dexter's defense the night of their 16th birthday party, telling their cousin Elliot to kiss off. Called him a douchebag. Went Twin Gangsta on his cocky ass.

Even though that was more than six months ago, re-telling that story is one of their favorite things to do in mixed company.

And they do it so well. So vividly.

So loudly.

The tips of Dexter's ears turn pink when Lucy throws her arms in the air, shouting, "We'll wait here while you finish him off!" The declaration is loud enough to be heard by everyone in the room.

My boyfriend groans. "Why do they insist on telling that story?" He runs a hand through his neatly combed hair, and my eyes follow his movements, trailing down the column of his neck to the exposed skin at his collar. "It's so embarrassing."

The top two buttons of his dress shirt, undone. For Dexter, this is as laid-back and casual as he gets. He does own tee shirts; I've seen them in his closet, and a few times on the weekends. But he likes to be dressed up. Pressed. Tidy.

It's my job to muss him up.

I press my mouth against his neck for a quick kiss, sniffing his deliciously male cologne. His woodsy shampoo. "Mmm, you smell good."

"Daphne, stop. You're going to make me—"

"—Hard?"

I love how open he is now; how uninhibited we are together. How honest and affectionate.

"Just hearing you say that word makes it worse." The low baritone of his voice gets lower, and he watches when I bite down on my lower lip, dragging my teeth back and forth.

I glance down the dark hallway off the living room, one eyebrow raised in thought. "Want to check out the spare bedroom?"

My meaning is clear.

Dexter swallows, his Adam's apple bobbing and eyes rapidly getting hazy behind the rim of his glasses. *Sexy*

Dexy indeed.

He gives a curt nod. *Yes.*

Grabs my hand. Hauls me down the dark corridor to the second door on the left, my body humming with need and anticipation with what's going to happen when we close the door to that dark spare room behind us.

Door locked, it's empty and pitch black.

Eyes straining, I can barely make out any furniture, let alone Dexter's fingers when he finds the tie of my emerald green wrap dress—the one I borrowed from Tabitha, fell into like with, and haven't given back. Wrapped around my waist, the soft cotton fits my body like a second skin, flattering my curves to perfection.

Large hands slide across the bare skin between the plunging wrap neckline, sliding into the cup of my bra, palm gently kneading my breast. Heaven. It feels like heaven.

Muffled sounds reverberate from the party outside, but we don't care.

"You're so sexy," he purrs in the dark, his lips finding purchase on my collarbone. "I've been wanting to touch you all night. Untie this dress and have my way with you."

"Yes," I breath into his mouth with a sigh; the mouth that I dream about each and every night; those lips that make all the aching in my body go away.

At some point I'm lifted onto the top of a dresser.

Fumbling hands find his belt buckle. Unzip his fly. Push the dark, dressy denim down his lean hips along with his navy boxer-briefs. Untie the sash around my waist. Push apart the cotton of my dress. Push aside my lacey, nude underwear.

My hands roam his torso, his taunt abs, his firm pecs.

I love his body.

I love his glasses.

I love his mind.

"I love you," I whisper when he pushes into me with a loud groan, condoms forgone when we became exclusive (not that there was any doubt we wouldn't be).

He thrusts once, then stills. "Did you just say that you love me?"

"Yes." I bob my head in the dark even though he can't see me. "Yes, yes, I love you." I wriggle my pelvis, hoping to urge him on.

He pulls out slowly. Pushes in slowly.

Again and again and again.

"God Daphne, oh god." He buries his nose in my hair, inhaling with a long drag. "I'm so in love with you."

Rocking. Pushing. Pulling.

The dresser hits the wall with every mad thrust, our loud moans and mutters drowned out only by the sound of party-goers in the next room. Vaguely I hear Tabitha's distinctive laugh, but my neck is rolling to the side and I'm drunk on the oxytocin surging through my body.

"I love you... oh! Oh god... mmmm..."

Bang.

Bang.

Bang. A picture on the wall behind my back falls, hits the hard wooden top of the dresser, and crashes to the ground with the telltale sound of broken glass.

We don't care.

We can't stop.

"Oh shit, oh fuck," Dexter grunts when we come at the same time. A wet kiss is planted at my temple, his chest heaving from his accelerated heart rate.

Then, after a lengthy silence, "How are we going to explain that broken whatever-that-is to Collin and Tabitha?"

He pulls away from my body, and I fumble to find the ties of my dress. "I'll probably just tell her the truth. I don't think she'll be mad."

I hear the sound of his zipper being pulled up, his belt being buckled. "Where's the damn light switch?"

Hands pat the wall, his voice fading as he nears the door.

The lights go on.

I blink rapidly to block out the blinding light, seeing nothing but…

Pink.

Pink, pink and more pink.

A white crib against the wall. A rocking chair with a little gray stuffed elephant in the corner. The letters "LKE" monogrammed in white, interlocking script in the center of the opposite, powder pink wall.

"Holy. Shit." Dexter breaths.

My mouth falls open, and I slap my hand over it to conceal my dread. "Oh my god. We just *sullied* a baby nursery with our fornicating!"

Which means…

"Oh my god. Tabitha is pregnant."

And not just pregnant—but *pregnant* pregnant. As in: she must be at least twenty weeks along if they already know the sex, have picked out a name, and decorated an entire nursery.

All the pieces of the puzzle slide into place: new bigger condo closer to the suburbs. Tabitha quitting her day job and writing from home. Collin taking that desk job at his firm so he wouldn't have to do any more traveling.

Her loose fitting shirt. Collin practically glued to her side all night, fawning all over her.

This party.

"Oh my god," I repeat with a horrified gasp. "Dexter. They're telling everyone tonight. That's what this is."

"*A baby*." We say the words together in wonderment.

"A girl," I breathe, the first twinge of envy planted inside my soul.

"Holy shit." He's rooted to the floor. "Collin is having a fucking baby."

He says it with such shock that I can't help but wonder…

"Do…" I gulp nervously, smoothing a hand down my dress to flatten the wrinkles out. "Do you want kids?"

I have to ask because, well. *I* do. Want kids, that is—so terribly. And I might only be twenty-five years old, but my biological clock has been ticking since the moment I met Dexter.

He is *it* for me.

"Of course I want kids."

I am *it* for him; I can see it in his eyes.

Hormones raging, our shy gazes meet.

Then our mouths clash.

"I love—" I murmur into the corner of his mouth.

"—You."

"We can't stay in here." One of us whispers.

"How are we going to—"

"—Look them in the eye?"

Eventually we come up for air, fixing our clothes, and my long hair. One last, long lingering kiss before together, we step through the door.

Dexter

Daphne loves me.

Yeah, we've been dating for the past few months, but I didn't actually think *she'd* be the one to blurt it out first; I assumed it would be me.

And now that I know, I can't stop watching her from across the room. My girlfriend. My best friend.

Loves me.

I watch as she flits from aunt to uncle, to college friends. I watch as she shimmies to the make-shift bar and pours herself a glass of wine. Grabs a beer from the ice bucket.

Watch as she makes her way towards me, this beautiful, gorgeous woman.

I push the glasses up my nose, shifting my focus to Collin as he leans in and whispers something in Tabitha's ear. She nods, biting her lower lip.

He clears his throat, preparing to speak, and I know exactly what's about to come next.

Daphne makes it to my side in time, handing me a beer bottle as Collin announces, "Everyone. Can I have your attention for a second?"

His arm goes protectively around Tabitha, and now that I know their secret, my eyes fly to her stomach. Straining to glean any signs of a baby bump, but not seeing one.

"First of all, thank you all for coming on such short notice. We have some exciting news that we didn't want to share online, and we're glad you could all make it." His voice breaks with a crack, emotion playing with every breath taken. "Tabitha and I... we..."

He looks at his parents.

Her parents.

Tabitha reaches between them and clasps his hand and I see him squeeze it.

Solidarity.

A team.

"Tabitha and I..." he begins again, clearing his throat and blowing out a puff of air. "We haven't been together long—not even a year, but when you know, you know, right?" The small gathered crowd chuckles. "For me, meeting Tabitha was love at first sight."

The room gives a collective '*Awwwww.*'

Collin looks over at me, and our eyes meet. I've known the guy almost my entire life and I can say with certainly that right now, he might sound confident—but he definitely looks like he's going to barf.

I give him a firm, *You got this, buddy* and an encouraging thumbs up.

Message received. "Anyway, we brought you here to tell you that... we're in love and, well. There's no easy way to say this, so... Mom. Dad. *Everyone*—we got married at the courthouse last week and... we're having a baby!"

For a second, no one moves.

The room is deafeningly silent.

"Surprise!" Tabitha radiates joy, hands flying to her

belly.

But then...

Both their mothers start to cry. All at once, everyone starts hugging. Excited chatter, a champagne bottle is uncorked and flies across the room. Wine is being poured.

It's a veritable love fest.

Greyson and Cal sidle up to Daphne and I get elbowed in the ribs by Collin's stunning kid sister.

She chuckles. "Well, since we're all sharing news, this might be a good time to go tell my parents Cal and I are moving in together this summer. There's no way they can get mad at us after *that* little announcement!"

With a laugh, they head off towards their parents, hand-in-hand.

"Wow, this whole night has been surreal," Daphne says beside me, leaning into me when I slide my arm around her waist. "First my friends all fall in love, then they're moving in together, then they're having babies..."

I plant a kiss on the top of her head. "We'll get there."

Her breath hitches. "Yeah?"

"Yeah."

She beams up at me, smiling wide. "I love you *so* much."

"I love you, too."

And you know what?

We do get there.

Exactly seventeen months and four days later.

Acknowledgements

I kept teasing my friend Christine (who does my proofreading, Facebook page, and basically helps manage my life) that i was going to start my acknowledgements with, "My Dearest Christine…." So. Here it goes.

My Dearest Christine, thank you for being part of the 'we.' I look forward to many adventures (and travels?!) together. Hint hint. Thanks for shedding that one tiny, solitary tear when you read the last lines of this book. <tear> It was an awkward moment for both of us, but it meant the world to me.

Thank you, as always, to my Beta's: Nikki Kroll, Christine, and M.E. Carter

Seriously. Without your feedback, the story is never quite as good, and I value your comments. Especially the ones that say: *Seriously? Are you trying to drive me nuts? OMG Stop using the word [fill in the blank]*

Thank you Shawn Garcia and Crystal Graham – who drove all the way to see me in Dallas, and trusted me with their purses while they worked the crowd. Er, I mean, book signing…

A huge thank you to Murphy Rae & Julie at JT Formatting, for well… *you know*.

Sorry I'm not more organized.

And as always, thank you, readers and family:
I write for you.

For more information about Sara Ney and her books, visit:

Facebook
www.facebook.com/saraneyauthor

Twitter
twitter.com/saraney

Goodreads
www.goodreads.com/author/show/9884194.Sara_H_Ney

Website
http://kissingincars.weebly.com

Other Titles by Sara

The Kiss and Make Up Series

Kissing in Cars
He Kissed Me First
A Kiss Like This

#ThreeLittleLies Series

Things Liars Say
Things Liars Hide
Things Liars Fake

With M.E. Carter

FriendTrip
FriendTrip: WeddedBliss (a FriendTrip novella)

Made in the USA
Columbia, SC
19 January 2018